The Head of Kay's

P. G. Wodehouse

The Head of Kay's

The present edition is a reproduction of previous publication of this classic work. Minor typographical errors may have been corrected without note, however, for an authentic reading experience the spelling, punctuation, and capitalization have been retained from the original text.

ISBN: 978-1-64799-322-1

CONTENTS

CONTENTS

I

MAINLY ABOUT FENN

"When we get licked tomorrow by half-a-dozen wickets," said Jimmy Silver, tilting his chair until the back touched the wall, "don't say I didn't warn you. If you fellows take down what I say from time to time in note-books, as you ought to do, you'll remember that I offered to give anyone odds that Kay's would out us in the final. I always said that a really hot man like Fenn was more good to a side than half-a-dozen ordinary men. He can do all the bowling and all the batting. All the fielding, too, in the slips."

Tea was just over at Blackburn's, and the bulk of the house had gone across to preparation in the school buildings. The prefects, as was their custom, lingered on to finish the meal at their leisure. These after-tea conversations were quite an institution at Blackburn's. The labours of the day were over, and the time for preparation for the morrow had not yet come. It would be time to be thinking of that in another hour. Meanwhile, a little relaxation might be enjoyed. Especially so as this was the last day but two of the summer term, and all necessity for working after tea had ceased with the arrival of the last lap of the examinations.

Silver was head of the house, and captain of its cricket team, which was nearing the end of its last match, the final for the inter-house cup, and—on paper—getting decidedly the worst of it. After riding in triumph over the School House, Bedell's, and Mulholland's, Blackburn's had met its next door neighbour, Kay's, in the final, and, to the surprise of the great majority of the school, was showing up badly. The match was affording one more example of how a team of average merit all through may sometimes fall before a one-man side. Blackburn's had the three last men on the list of the first eleven, Silver, Kennedy, and Challis, and at least nine of its representatives had the reputation of being able to knock up a useful twenty or thirty at any time. Kay's, on the other hand, had one man, Fenn. After him the tail started. But Fenn was such an exceptional all-round man that, as Silver had said, he was as good as half-a-dozen of the Blackburn's team, equally formidable whether

1

batting or bowling—he headed the school averages at both. He was one of those batsmen who seem to know exactly what sort of ball you are going to bowl before it leaves your hand, and he could hit like another Jessop. As for his bowling, he bowled left hand—always a puzzling eccentricity to an undeveloped batsman—and could send them down very fast or very slow, as he thought best, and it was hard to see which particular brand he was going to serve up before it was actually in mid-air.

But it is not necessary to enlarge on his abilities. The figures against his name in Wisden prove a good deal. The fact that he had steered Kay's through into the last round of the house-matches proves still more. It was perfectly obvious to everyone that, if only you could get Fenn out for under ten, Kay's total for that innings would be nearer twenty than forty. They were an appalling side. But then no house bowler had as yet succeeded in getting Fenn out for under ten. In the six innings he had played in the competition up to date, he had made four centuries, an eighty, and a seventy.

Kennedy, the second prefect at Blackburn's, paused in the act of grappling with the remnant of a pot of jam belonging to some person unknown, to reply to Silver's remarks.

"We aren't beaten yet," he said, in his solid way. Kennedy's chief characteristics were solidity, and an infinite capacity for taking pains. Nothing seemed to tire or discourage him. He kept pegging away till he arrived. The ordinary person, for instance, would have considered the jam-pot, on which he was then engaged, an empty jam-pot. Kennedy saw that there was still a strawberry (or it may have been a section of a strawberry) at the extreme end, and he meant to have that coy vegetable if he had to squeeze the pot to get at it. To take another instance, all the afternoon of the previous day he had bowled patiently at Fenn while the latter lifted every other ball into space. He had been taken off three times, and at every fresh attack he had plodded on doggedly, until at last, as he had expected, the batsman had misjudged a straight one, and he had bowled him all over his wicket. Kennedy generally managed to get there sooner or later.

"It's no good chucking the game up simply because we're in a tight place," he said, bringing the spoon to the surface at last with the section of strawberry adhering to the end of it. "That sort of thing's awfully feeble."

2

"He calls me feeble!" shouted Jimmy Silver. "By James, I've put a man to sleep for less."

It was one of his amusements to express himself from time to time in a melodramatic fashion, sometimes accompanying his words with suitable gestures. It was on one of these occasions—when he had assumed at a moment's notice the role of the "Baffled Despot", in an argument with Kennedy in his study on the subject of the house football team—that he broke what Mr Blackburn considered a valuable door with a poker. Since then he had moderated his transports.

"They've got to make seventy-nine," said Kennedy.

Challis, the other first eleven man, was reading a green scoring-book.

"I don't think Kay's ought to have the face to stick the cup up in their dining-room," he said, "considering the little they've done to win it. If they do win it, that is. Still, as they made two hundred first innings, they ought to be able to knock off seventy-nine. But I was saying that the pot ought to go to Fenn. Lot the rest of the team had to do with it. Blackburn's, first innings, hundred and fifty-one; Fenn, eight for forty-nine. Kay's, two hundred and one; Fenn, a hundred and sixty-four not out. Second innings, Blackburn's hundred and twenty-eight; Fenn ten for eighty. Bit thick, isn't it? I suppose that's what you'd call a one-man team."

Williams, one of the other prefects, who had just sat down at the piano for the purpose of playing his one tune—a cake-walk, of which, through constant practice, he had mastered the rudiments—spoke over his shoulder to Silver.

"I tell you what, Jimmy," he said, "you've probably lost us the pot by getting your people to send brother Billy to Kay's. If he hadn't kept up his wicket yesterday, Fenn wouldn't have made half as many."

When his young brother had been sent to Eckleton two terms before, Jimmy Silver had strongly urged upon his father the necessity of placing him in some house other than Blackburn's. He felt that a head of a house, even of so orderly and perfect a house as Blackburn's, has enough worries without being saddled with a small brother. And on the previous afternoon young Billy Silver, going in eighth wicket for Kay's, had put a solid bat in front of everything for

3

the space of one hour, in the course of which he made ten runs and Fenn sixty. By scoring odd numbers off the last ball of each over, Fenn had managed to secure the majority of the bowling in the most masterly way.

"These things will happen," said Silver, resignedly. "We Silvers, you know, can't help making runs. Come on, Williams, let's have that tune, and get it over."

Williams obliged. It was a classic piece called "The Coon Band Contest", remarkable partly for a taking melody, partly for the vast possibilities of noise which it afforded. Williams made up for his failure to do justice to the former by a keen appreciation of the latter. He played the piece through again, in order to correct the mistakes he had made at his first rendering of it. Then he played it for the third time to correct a new batch of errors.

"I should like to hear Fenn play that," said Challis. "You're awfully good, you know, Williams, but he might do it better still."

"Get him to play it as an encore at the concert," said Williams, starting for the fourth time.

The talented Fenn was also a musician,—not a genius at the piano, as he was at cricket, but a sufficiently sound performer for his age, considering that he had not made a special study of it. He was to play at the school concert on the following day.

"I believe Fenn has an awful time at Kay's," said Jimmy Silver. "It must be a fair sort of hole, judging from the specimens you see crawling about in Kay caps. I wish I'd known my people were sending young Billy there. I'd have warned them. I only told them not to sling him in here. I had no idea they'd have picked Kay's."

"Fenn was telling me the other day," said Kennedy, "that being in Kay's had spoiled his whole time at the school. He always wanted to come to Blackburn's, only there wasn't room that particular term. Bad luck, wasn't it? I don't think he found it so bad before he became head of the house. He didn't come into contact with Kay so much. But now he finds that he can't do a thing without Kay buzzing round and interfering."

"I wonder," said Jimmy Silver, thoughtfully, "if that's why he bowls so fast. To work it off, you know."

In the course of a beautiful innings of fifty-three that afternoon, the captain of Blackburn's had received two of Fenn's speediest on the same spot just above the pad in rapid succession, and he now hobbled painfully when he moved about.

The conversation that evening had dealt so largely with Fenn—the whole school, indeed, was talking of nothing but his great attempt to win the cricket cup single-handed—that Kennedy, going out into the road for a breather before the rest of the boarders returned from preparation, made his way to Kay's to see if Fenn was imitating his example, and taking the air too.

He found him at Kay's gate, and they strolled towards the school buildings together. Fenn was unusually silent.

"Well?" said Kennedy, after a minute had passed without a remark.

"Well, what?"

"What's up?"

Fenn laughed what novelists are fond of calling a mirthless laugh.

"Oh, I don't know," he said; "I'm sick of this place."

Kennedy inspected his friend's face anxiously by the light of the lamp over the school gate. There was no mistake about it. Fenn certainly did look bad. His face always looked lean and craggy, but tonight there was a difference. He looked used up.

"Fagged?" asked Kennedy.

"No. Sick."

"What about?"

"Everything. I wish you could come into Kay's for a bit just to see what it's like. Then you'd understand. At present I don't suppose you've an idea of it. I'd like to write a book on 'Kay Day by Day'. I'd have plenty to put in it."

"What's he been doing?"

"Oh, nothing out of the ordinary run. It's the fact that he's always at it that does me. You get a houseful of—well, you know the sort of chap the average Kayite is. They'd keep me busy even if I were

5

allowed a free hand. But I'm not. Whenever I try and keep order and stop things a bit, out springs the man Kay from nowhere, and takes the job out of my hands, makes a ghastly mess of everything, and retires purring. Once in every three times, or thereabouts, he slangs me in front of the kids for not keeping order. I'm glad this is the end of the term. I couldn't stand it much longer. Hullo, here come the chaps from prep. We'd better be getting back."

II

AN EVENING AT KAY'S

They turned, and began to walk towards the houses. Kennedy felt miserable. He never allowed himself to be put out, to any great extent, by his own worries, which, indeed, had not been very numerous up to the present, but the misfortunes of his friends always troubled him exceedingly. When anything happened to him personally, he found the discomfort of being in a tight place largely counterbalanced by the excitement of trying to find a way out. But the impossibility of helping Fenn in any way depressed him.

"It must be awful," he said, breaking the silence.

"It is," said Fenn, briefly.

"But haven't the house-matches made any difference? Blackburn's always frightfully bucked when the house does anything. You can do anything you like with him if you lift a cup. I should have thought Kay would have been all right when he saw you knocking up centuries, and getting into the final, and all that sort of thing."

Fenn laughed.

"Kay!" he said. "My dear man, he doesn't know. I don't suppose he's got the remotest idea that we are in the final at all, or, if he has, he doesn't understand what being in the final means."

"But surely he'll be glad if you lick us tomorrow?" asked Kennedy. Such indifference on the part of a house-master respecting the fortunes of his house seemed to him, having before him the bright example of Mr Blackburn, almost incredible.

"I don't suppose so," said Fenn. "Or, if he is, I'll bet he doesn't show it. He's not like Blackburn. I wish he was. Here he comes, so perhaps we'd better talk about something else."

The vanguard of the boys returning from preparation had passed them, and they were now standing at the gate of the house. As Fenn spoke, a little, restless-looking man in cap and gown came up. His clean-shaven face wore an expression of extreme alertness—the sort of look a ferret wears as he slips in at the mouth of a rabbit-hole. A doctor, called upon to sum up Mr Kay at a glance, would probably have said that he suffered from nerves, which would have been a perfectly correct diagnosis, though none of the members of his house put his manners and customs down to that cause. They considered that the methods he pursued in the management of the house were the outcome of a naturally malignant disposition. This was, however, not the case. There is no reason to suppose that Mr Kay did not mean well. But there is no doubt that he was extremely fussy. And fussiness—with the possible exceptions of homicidal mania and a taste for arson—is quite the worst characteristic it is possible for a house-master to possess.

He caught sight of Fenn and Kennedy at the gate, and stopped in his stride.

"What are you doing here, Fenn?" he asked, with an abruptness which brought a flush to the latter's face. "Why are you outside the house?"

Kennedy began to understand why it was that his friend felt so strongly on the subject of his house-master. If this was the sort of thing that happened every day, no wonder that there was dissension in the house of Kay. He tried to imagine Blackburn speaking in that way to Jimmy Silver or himself, but his imagination was unequal to the task. Between Mr Blackburn and his prefects there existed a perfect understanding. He relied on them to see that order was kept, and they acted accordingly. Fenn, by the exercise of considerable self-control, had always been scrupulously polite to Mr Kay.

"I came out to get some fresh air before lock-up, sir," he replied.

"Well, go in. Go in at once. I cannot allow you to be outside the house at this hour. Go indoors directly."

Kennedy expected a scene, but Fenn took it quite quietly.

"Good night, Kennedy," he said.

"So long," said Kennedy.

Fenn caught his eye, and smiled painfully. Then he turned and went into the house.

Mr Kay's zeal for reform was apparently still unsatisfied. He directed his batteries towards Kennedy.

"Go to your house at once, Kennedy. You have no business out here at this time."

This, thought Kennedy, was getting a bit too warm. Mr Kay might do as he pleased with his own house, but he was hanged if he was going to trample on him.

"Mr Blackburn is my house-master, sir," he said with great respect.

Mr Kay stared.

"My house-master," continued Kennedy with gusto, slightly emphasising the first word, "knows that I always go out just before lock-up, and he has no objection."

And, to emphasise this point, he walked towards the school buildings again. For a moment it seemed as if Mr Kay intended to call him back, but he thought better of it. Mr Blackburn, in normal circumstances a pacific man, had one touchy point—his house. He resented any interference with its management, and was in the habit of saying so. Mr Kay remembered one painful scene in the Masters' Common Room, when he had ventured to let fall a few well-meant hints as to how a house should be ruled. Really, he had thought Blackburn would have choked. Better, perhaps, to leave him to look after his own affairs.

So Mr Kay followed Fenn indoors, and Kennedy, having watched him vanish, made his way to Blackburn's.

Quietly as Fenn had taken the incident at the gate, it nevertheless rankled. He read prayers that night in a distinctly unprayerful mood. It seemed to him that it would be lucky if he could get through to the end of the term before Mr Kay applied that last straw which does not break the backs of camels only. Eight weeks' holiday, with plenty of cricket, would brace him up for another term. And he had been invited to play for the county against Middlesex four days after the holidays began. That should have been a soothing thought. But it really seemed to make matters worse. It was hard that a man who on Monday would be bowling against Warner and Beldam, or standing up to Trott and Hearne, should on the preceding Tuesday be sent indoors like a naughty child by a man who stood five-feet-one in his boots, and was devoid of any sort of merit whatever.

9

It seemed to him that it would help him to sleep peacefully that night if he worked off a little of his just indignation upon somebody. There was a noise going on in the fags' room. There always was at Kay's. It was not a particularly noisy noise—considering; but it had better be stopped. Badly as Kay had treated him, he remembered that he was head of the house, and as such it behoved him to keep order in the house.

He went downstairs, and, on arriving on the scene of action, found that the fags were engaged upon spirited festivities, partly in honour of the near approach of the summer holidays, partly because— miracles barred—the house was going on the morrow to lift the cricket-cup. There were a good many books flying about, and not a few slippers. There was a confused mass rolling in combat on the floor, and the table was occupied by a scarlet-faced individual, who passed the time by kicking violently at certain hands, which were endeavouring to drag him from his post, and shrieking frenzied abuse at the owners of the said hands. It was an animated scene, and to a deaf man might have been most enjoyable.

Fenn's appearance was the signal for a temporary suspension of hostilities.

"What the dickens is all this row about?" he inquired.

No one seemed ready at the moment with a concise explanation. There was an awkward silence. One or two of the weaker spirits even went so far as to sit down and begin to read. All would have been well but for a bright idea which struck some undiscovered youth at the back of the room.

"Three cheers for Fenn!" observed this genial spirit, in no uncertain voice.

The idea caught on. It was just what was wanted to give a finish to the evening's festivities. Fenn had done well by the house. He had scored four centuries and an eighty, and was going to knock off the runs against Blackburn's tomorrow off his own bat. Also, he had taken eighteen wickets in the final house-match. Obviously Fenn was a person deserving of all encouragement. It would be a pity to let him think that his effort had passed unnoticed by the fags' room. Happy thought! Three cheers and one more, and then "He's a jolly good fellow", to wind up with.

It was while those familiar words, "It's a way we have in the public

10

scho-o-o-o-l-s", were echoing through the room in various keys, that a small and energetic form brushed past Fenn as he stood in the doorway, vainly trying to stop the fags' choral efforts.

It was Mr Kay.

The singing ceased gradually, very gradually. It was some time before Mr Kay could make himself heard. But after a couple of minutes there was a lull, and the house-master's address began to be audible.

"... unendurable noise. What is the meaning of it? I will not have it. Do you hear? It is disgraceful. Every boy in this room will write me two hundred lines by tomorrow evening. It is abominable, Fenn." He wheeled round towards the head of the house. "Fenn, I am surprised at you standing here and allowing such a disgraceful disturbance to go on. Really, if you cannot keep order better—It is disgraceful, disgraceful."

Mr Kay shot out of the room. Fenn followed in his wake, and the procession made its way to the house-masters' study. It had been a near thing, but the last straw had arrived before the holidays.

Mr Kay wheeled round as he reached his study door.

"Well, Fenn?"

Fenn said nothing.

"Have you anything you wish to say, Fenn?"

"I thought you might have something to say to me, sir."

"I do not understand you, Fenn."

"I thought you might wish to apologise for slanging me in front of the fags."

It is wonderful what a difference the last straw will make in one's demeanour to a person.

"Apologise! I think you forget whom it is you are speaking to."

When a master makes this well-worn remark, the wise youth realises that the time has come to close the conversation. All Fenn's prudence, however, had gone to the four winds.

11

"If you wanted to tell me I was not fit to be head of the house, you needn't have done it before a roomful of fags. How do you think I can keep order in the house if you do that sort of thing?"

Mr Kay overcame his impulse to end the interview abruptly in order to put in a thrust.

"You do not keep order in the house, Fenn," he said, acidly.

"I do when I am not interfered with."

"You will be good enough to say 'sir' when you speak to me, Fenn," said Mr Kay, thereby scoring another point. In the stress of the moment, Fenn had not noticed the omission.

He was silenced. And before he could recover himself, Mr Kay was in his study, and there was a closed, forbidding door between them.

And as he stared at it, it began slowly to dawn upon Fenn that he had not shown up to advantage in the recent interview. In a word, he had made a fool of himself.

III

THE FINAL HOUSE-MATCH

Blackburn's took the field at three punctually on the following afternoon, to play out the last act of the final house-match. They were not without some small hope of victory, for curious things happen at cricket, especially in the fourth innings of a match. And runs are admitted to be easier saved than made. Yet seventy-nine seemed an absurdly small score to try and dismiss a team for, and in view of the fact that that team contained a batsman like Fenn, it seemed smaller still. But Jimmy Silver, resolutely as he had declared victory impossible to his intimate friends, was not the man to depress his team by letting it become generally known that he considered Blackburn's chances small.

"You must work like niggers in the field," he said; "don't give away a run. Seventy-nine isn't much to make, but if we get Fenn out for a few, they won't come near it."

He did not add that in his opinion Fenn would take very good care that he did not get out for a few. It was far more likely that he would make that seventy-nine off his own bat in a dozen overs.

"You'd better begin, Kennedy," he continued, "from the top end. Place your men where you want 'em. I should have an extra man in the deep, if I were you. That's where Fenn kept putting them last innings. And you'll want a short leg, only for goodness sake keep them off the leg-side if you can. It's a safe four to Fenn every time if you don't. Look out, you chaps. Man in."

Kay's first pair were coming down the pavilion steps.

Challis, going to his place at short slip, called Silver's attention to a remarkable fact.

"Hullo," he said, "why isn't Fenn coming in first?"

"What! By Jove, nor he is. That's queer. All the better for us. You might get a bit finer, Challis, in case they snick 'em."

13

Wayburn, who had accompanied Fenn to the wicket at the beginning of Kay's first innings, had now for his partner one Walton, a large, unpleasant-looking youth, said to be a bit of a bruiser, and known to be a black sheep. He was one of those who made life at Kay's so close an imitation of an Inferno. His cricket was of a rustic order. He hit hard and high. When allowed to do so, he hit often. But, as a rule, he left early, a prey to the slips or deep fields. Today was no exception to that rule.

Kennedy's first ball was straight and medium-paced. It was a little too short, however, and Walton, letting go at it with a semi-circular sweep like the drive of a golfer, sent it soaring over mid-on's head and over the boundary. Cheers from the pavilion.

Kennedy bowled his second ball with the same purposeful air, and Walton swept at it as before. There was a click, and Jimmy Silver, who was keeping wicket, took the ball comfortably on a level with his chin.

"How's that?"

The umpire's hand went up, and Walton went out—reluctantly, murmuring legends of how he had not gone within a yard of the thing.

It was only when the next batsman who emerged from the pavilion turned out to be his young brother and not Fenn, that Silver began to see that something was wrong. It was conceivable that Fenn might have chosen to go in first wicket down instead of opening the batting, but not that he should go in second wicket. If Kay's were to win it was essential that he should begin to bat as soon as possible. Otherwise there might be no time for him to knock off the runs. However good a batsman is, he can do little if no one can stay with him.

There was no time to question the newcomer. He must control his curiosity until the fall of the next wicket.

"Man in," he said.

Billy Silver was in many ways a miniature edition of his brother, and he carried the resemblance into his batting. The head of Blackburn's was stylish, and took no risks. His brother had not yet developed a style, but he was very settled in his mind on the subject of risks.

14

There was no tempting him with half-volleys and long-hops. His motto was defence, not defiance. He placed a straight bat in the path of every ball, and seemed to consider his duty done if he stopped it.

The remainder of the over was, therefore, quiet. Billy played Kennedy's fastest like a book, and left the more tempting ones alone.

Challis's first over realised a single, Wayburn snicking him to leg. The first ball of Kennedy's second over saw him caught at the wicket, as Walton had been.

"Every time a coconut," said Jimmy Silver complacently, as he walked to the other end. "We're a powerful combination, Kennedy. Where's Fenn? Does anybody know? Why doesn't he come in?"

Billy Silver, seated on the grass by the side of the crease, fastening the top strap of one of his pads, gave tongue with the eagerness of the well-informed man.

"What, don't you know?" he said. "Why, there's been an awful row. Fenn won't be able to play till four o'clock. I believe he and Kay had a row last night, and he cheeked Kay, and the old man's given him a sort of extra. I saw him going over to the School House, and I heard him tell Wayburn that he wouldn't be able to play till four."

The effect produced by this communication would be most fittingly expressed by the word "sensation" in brackets. It came as a complete surprise to everyone. It seemed to knock the bottom out of the whole match. Without Fenn the thing would be a farce. Kay's would have no chance.

"What a worm that man is," said Kennedy. "Do you know, I had a sort of idea Fenn wouldn't last out much longer. Kay's been ragging him all the term. I went round to see him last night, and Kay behaved like a bounder then. I expect Fenn had it out with him when they got indoors. What a beastly shame, though."

"Beastly," agreed Jimmy Silver. "Still, it can't be helped. The sins of the house-master are visited on the house. I'm afraid it will be our painful duty to wipe the floor with Kay's this day. Speaking at a venture, I should say that we have got them where the hair's short. Yea. Even on toast, if I may be allowed to use the expression. Who is

15

this coming forth now? Curtis, or me old eyes deceive me. And is not Curtis's record score three, marred by ten chances? Indeed yes. A fastish yorker should settle Curtis's young hash. Try one."

Kennedy followed the recipe. A ball later the middle and leg stumps were lying in picturesque attitudes some yards behind the crease, and Curtis was beginning that "sad, unending walk to the pavilion", thinking, with the poet,

"Thou vast not made to play, infernal ball!"

Blackburn's non-combatants, dotted round the boundary, shrieked their applause. Three wickets had fallen for five runs, and life was worth living. Kay's were silent and gloomy.

Billy Silver continued to occupy one end in an immovable manner, but at the other there was no monotony. Man after man came in, padded and gloved, and looking capable of mighty things. They took guard, patted the ground lustily, as if to make it plain that they were going to stand no nonsense, settled their caps over their eyes, and prepared to receive the ball. When it came it usually took a stump or two with it before it stopped. It was a procession such as the school grounds had not often seen. As the tenth man walked from the pavilion, four sounded from the clock over the Great Hall, and five minutes later the weary eyes of the supporters of Kay's were refreshed by the sight of Fenn making his way to the arena from the direction of the School House.

Just as he arrived on the scene, Billy Silver's defence broke down. One of Challis's slows, which he had left alone with the idea that it was going to break away to the off, came in quickly instead, and removed a bail. Billy Silver had only made eight; but, as the full score, including one bye, was only eighteen, this was above the average, and deserved the applause it received.

Fenn came in in the unusual position of eleventh man, with an expression on his face that seemed to suggest that he meant business. He was curiously garbed. Owing to the shortness of the interval allowed him for changing, he had only managed to extend his cricket costume as far as white buckskin boots. He wore no pads or gloves. But even in the face of these sartorial deficiencies, he looked like a cricketer. The field spread out respectfully, and Jimmy Silver moved a man from the slips into the country.

There were three more balls of Challis's over, for Billy Silver's collapse had occurred at the third delivery. Fenn mistimed the first. Two hours' writing indoors does not improve the eye. The ball missed the leg stump by an inch.

About the fifth ball he made no mistake. He got the full face of the bat to it, and it hummed past coverpoint to the boundary. The last of the over he put to leg for three.

A remarkable last-wicket partnership now took place, remarkable not so much for tall scoring as for the fact that one of the partners did not receive a single ball from beginning to end of it, with the exception of the one that bowled him. Fenn seemed to be able to do what he pleased with the bowling. Kennedy he played with a shade more respect than the others, but he never failed to score a three or a single off the last ball of each of his overs. The figures on the telegraph-board rose from twenty to thirty, from thirty to forty, from forty to fifty. Williams went on at the lower end instead of Challis, and Fenn made twelve off his first over. The pavilion was filled with howling enthusiasts, who cheered every hit in a frenzy.

Jimmy Silver began to look worried. He held a hasty consultation with Kennedy. The telegraph-board now showed the figures 60-9-8.

"This won't do," said Silver. "It would be too foul to get licked after having nine of them out for eighteen. Can't you manage to keep Fenn from scoring odd figures off the last ball of your over? If only that kid at the other end would get some of the bowling, we should do it."

"I'll try," said Kennedy, and walked back to begin his over.

Fenn reached his fifty off the third ball. Seventy went up on the board. Ten more and Kay's would have the cup. The fourth ball was too good to hit. Fenn let it pass. The fifth he drove to the on. It was a big hit, but there was a fieldsman in the neighbourhood. Still, it was an easy two. But to Kennedy's surprise Fenn sent his partner back after they had run a single. Even the umpire was surprised. Fenn's policy was so obvious that it was strange to see him thus deliberately allow his partner to take a ball.

"That's not over, you know, Fenn," said the umpire—Lang, of the School House, a member of the first eleven.

Fenn looked annoyed. He had miscounted the balls, and now his partner, who had no pretensions to be considered a bat, would have to face Kennedy.

17

That mistake lost Kay's the match.

Impossible as he had found it to defeat Fenn, Kennedy had never lost his head or his length. He was bowling fully as well as he had done at the beginning of the innings.

The last ball of the over beat the batsman all the way. He scooped blindly forward, missed it by a foot, and the next moment the off stump lay flat. Blackburn's had won by seven runs.

IV

HARMONY AND DISCORD

What might be described as a mixed reception awaited the players as they left the field. The pavilion and the parts about the pavilion rails were always packed on the last day of a final house-match, and even in normal circumstances there was apt to be a little sparring between the juniors of the two houses which had been playing for the cup. In the present case, therefore, it was not surprising that Kay's fags took the defeat badly. The thought that Fenn's presence at the beginning of the innings, instead of at the end, would have made all the difference between a loss and a victory, maddened them. The crowd that seethed in front of the pavilion was a turbulent one.

For a time the operation of chairing Fenn up the steps occupied the active minds of the Kayites. When he had disappeared into the first eleven room, they turned their attention in other directions. Caustic and uncomplimentary remarks began to fly to and fro between the representatives of Kay's and Blackburn's. It is not known who actually administered the first blow. But, when Fenn came out of the pavilion with Kennedy and Silver, he found a stirring battle in progress. The members of the other houses who had come to look on at the match stood in knots, and gazed with approval at the efforts of Kay's and Blackburn's juniors to wipe each other off the face of the earth. The air was full of shrill battle-cries, varied now and then by a smack or a thud, as some young but strenuous fist found a billet. The fortune of war seemed to be distributed equally so far, and the combatants were just warming to their work.

"Look here," said Kennedy, "we ought to stop this."

"What's the good," said Fenn, without interest. "It pleases them, and doesn't hurt anybody else."

"All the same," observed Jimmy Silver, moving towards the nearest group of combatants, "free fights aren't quite the thing, somehow. For, children, you should never let your angry passions rise; your little hands were never made to tear each other's eyes. Dr Watts' Advice to Young Pugilists. Drop it, you little beasts."

He separated two heated youths who were just beginning a fourth round. The rest of the warriors, seeing Silver and the others, called a truce, and Silver, having read a sort of Riot Act, moved on. The juniors of the beaten house, deciding that it would be better not to resume hostilities, consoled themselves by giving three groans for Mr Kay.

"What happened after I left you last night, Fenn?" asked Kennedy.

"Oh, I had one of my usual rows with Kay, only rather worse than usual. I said one or two things he didn't like, and today the old man sent for me and told me to come to his room from two till four. Kay had run me in for being 'grossly rude'. Listen to those kids. What a row they're making!"

"It's a beastly shame," said Kennedy despondently.

At the school shop Morrell, of Mulholland's, met them. He had been spending the afternoon with a rug and a novel on the hills at the back of the school, and he wanted to know how the final house-match had gone. Blackburn's had beaten Mulholland's in one of the early rounds. Kennedy explained what had happened.

"We should have lost if Fenn had turned up earlier," he said. "He had a row with Kay, and Kay gave him a sort of extra between two and four."

Fenn, busily occupied with an ice, added no comment of his own to this plain tale.

"Rough luck," said Morrell. "What's all that row out in the field?"

"That's Kay's kids giving three groans for Kay," explained Silver. "At least, they started with the idea of giving three groans. They've got up to about three hundred by this time. It seems to have fascinated them. They won't leave off. There's no school rule against groaning in the grounds, and they mean to groan till the end of the term. Personally, I like the sound. But then, I'm fond of music."

Morrell's face beamed with sudden pleasure. "I knew there was something I wanted to tell you," he said, "only I couldn't remember what. Your saying you're fond of music reminds me. Mulholland's crocked himself, and won't be able to turn out for the concert."

"What!" cried Kennedy. "How did it happen? What's he done?"

20

Mr Mulholland was the master who looked after the music of the school, a fine cricketer and keen sportsman. Had nothing gone wrong, he would have conducted at the concert that night.

"I heard it from the matron at our place," said Morrell. "She's full of it. Mulholland was batting at the middle net, and somebody else—I forget who—was at the one next to it on the right. The bowler sent down a long-hop to leg, and this Johnny had a smack at it, and sent it slap through the net, and it got Mulholland on the side of the head. He was stunned for a bit, but he's getting all right again now. But he won't be able to conduct tonight. Rather bad luck on the man, especially as he's so keen on the concert."

"Who's going to sub for him?" asked Silver. "Perhaps they'll scratch the show," suggested Kennedy.

"Oh, no," said Morrell, "it's all right. Kay is going to conduct. He's often done it at choir practices when Mulholland couldn't turn up."

Fenn put down his empty saucer with an emphatic crack on the counter.

"If Kay's going to run the show, I'm hanged if I turn up," he said.

"My dear chap, you can't get out of it now," said Kennedy anxiously. He did not want to see Fenn plunging into any more strife with the authorities this term.

"Think of the crowned heads who are coming to hear you," pleaded Jimmy Silver. "Think of the nobility and gentry. Think of me. You must play."

"Ah, there you are, Fenn."

Mr Kay had bustled in in his energetic way.

Fenn said nothing. He was there. It was idle to deny it.

"I thought I should find you here. Yes, I wanted to see you about the concert tonight. Mr Mulholland has met with an unfortunate accident, and I am looking after the entertainment in his place. Come with me and play over your piece. I should like to see that you are perfect in it. Dear me, dear me, what a noise those boys are making. Why are they behaving in that extraordinary way, I wonder!"

21

Kay's juniors had left the pavilion, and were trooping back to their house. At the present moment they were passing the school shop, and their tuneful voices floated in through the open window.

"This is very unusual. Why, they seem to be boys in my house. They are groaning."

"I think they are a little upset at the result of the match, sir," said Jimmy Silver suavely. "Fenn did not arrive, for some reason, till the end of the innings, so Mr Blackburn's won. The wicket was good, but a little fiery."

"Thank you, Silver," replied Mr Kay with asperity. "When I require explanations I will ask for them."

He darted out of the shop, and a moment later they heard him pouring out a flood of recriminations on the groaning fags.

"There was once a man who snubbed me," said Jimmy Silver. "They buried him at Brookwood. Well, what are you going to do, Fenn? Going to play tonight? Harkee, boy. Say but the word, and I will beard this tyrant to his face."

Fenn rose.

"Yes," he said briefly, "I shall play. You'd better turn up. I think you'll enjoy it."

Silver said that no human power should keep him away.

The School concert was always one of the events of the summer term. There was a concert at the end of the winter term, too, but it was not so important. To a great many of those present the summer concert marked, as it were, the last flutter of their school life. On the morrow they would be Old Boys, and it behoved them to extract as much enjoyment from the function as they could. Under Mr Mullholland's rule the concert had become a very flourishing institution. He aimed at a high standard, and reached it. There was more than a touch of the austere about the music. A glance at the programme was enough to show the lover of airs of the trashy, clashy order that this was no place for him. Most of the items were serious. When it was thought necessary to introduce a lighter touch, some staidly rollicking number was inserted, some song that was saved—in spite of a catchy tune—by a halo of antiquity. Anything modern was taboo, unless it were the work of Gotsuchakoff,

Thingummyowsky, or some other eminent foreigner. Foreign origin made it just possible.

The school prefects lurked during the performance at the doors and at the foot of the broad stone steps that led to the Great Hall. It was their duty to supply visitors with programmes.

Jimmy Silver had foregathered with Kennedy, Challis, and Williams at the junior door. The hall was full now, and their labours consequently at an end.

"Pretty good 'gate'," said Silver, looking in through the open door. "It must be warm up in the gallery."

Across the further end of the hall a dais had been erected. On this the bulk of the school sat, leaving the body of the hall to the crowned heads, nobility, and gentry to whom Silver had referred in his conversation with Fenn.

"It always is warm in the gallery," said Challis. "I lost about two stone there every concert when I was a kid. We simply used to sit and melt."

"And I tell you what," broke in Silver, "it's going to get warmer before the end of the show. Do you notice that all Kay's house are sitting in a lump at the back. I bet they're simply spoiling for a row. Especially now Kay's running the concert. There's going to be a hot time in the old town tonight—you see if there isn't. Hark at 'em."

The choir had just come to the end of a little thing of Handel's. There was no reason to suppose that the gallery appreciated Handel. Nevertheless, they were making a deafening noise. Clouds of dust rose from the rhythmical stamping of many feet. The noise was loudest and the dust thickest by the big window, beneath which sat the men from Kay's. Things were warming up.

The gallery, with one last stamp which nearly caused the dais to collapse, quieted down. The masters in the audience looked serious. One or two of the visitors glanced over their shoulders with a smile. How excited the dear boys were at the prospect of holidays! Young blood! Young blood! Boys would be boys.

The concert continued. Half-way through the programme there was a ten minutes' interval. Fenn's pianoforte solo was the second item of the second half.

23

He mounted the platform amidst howls of delight from the gallery. Applause at the Eckleton concerts was granted more for services in the playing-fields than merit as a musician. Kubelik or Paderewski would have been welcomed with a few polite handclaps. A man in the eleven or fifteen was certain of two minutes' unceasing cheers.

"Evidently one of their heroes, my dear," said Paterfamilias to Materfamilias. "I suppose he has won a scholarship at the University."

Paterfamilias' mind was accustomed to run somewhat upon scholarships at the University. What the school wanted was a batting average of forty odd or a bowling analysis in single figures.

Fenn played the "Moonlight Sonata". A trained musical critic would probably have found much to cavil at in his rendering of the piece, but it was undoubtedly good for a public school player. Of course he was encored. The gallery would have encored him if he had played with one finger, three mistakes to every bar.

"I told Fenn," said Jimmy Silver, "if he got an encore, that he ought to play the—My aunt! He is!"

Three runs and half-a-dozen crashes, and there was no further room for doubt. Fenn was playing the "Coon Band Contest".

"He's gone mad," gasped Kennedy.

Whether he had or not, it is certain that the gallery had. All the evening they had been stewing in an atmosphere like that of the inner room of a Turkish bath, and they were ready for anything. It needed but a trifle to set them off. The lilt of that unspeakable Yankee melody supplied that trifle. Kay's malcontents, huddled in their seats by the window, were the first to break out. Feet began to stamp in time to the music—softly at first, then more loudly. The wooden dais gave out the sound like a drum.

Other rioters joined in from the right. The noise spread through the gallery as a fire spreads through gorse. Soon three hundred pairs of well-shod feet were rising and falling. Somebody began to whistle. Everybody whistled. Mr Kay was on his feet, gesticulating wildly. His words were lost in the uproar.

For five minutes the din prevailed. Then, with a final crash, Fenn finished. He got up from the music-stool, bowed, and walked back

24

to his place by the senior door. The musical efforts of the gallery changed to a storm of cheering and clapping.

The choir rose to begin the next piece.

Still the noise continued.

People began to leave the Hall—in ones and twos first, then in a steady stream which blocked the doorways. It was plain to the dullest intelligence that if there was going to be any more concert, it would have to be performed in dumb show. Mr Kay flung down his baton.

The visitors had left by now, and the gallery was beginning to follow their example, howling as it went.

"Well," said Jimmy Silver cheerfully, as he went with Kennedy down the steps, "I think we may call that a record. By my halidom, there'll be a row about this later on."

V

CAMP

With the best intentions in the world, however, a headmaster cannot make a row about a thing unless he is given a reasonable amount of time to make it in. The concert being on the last evening of term, there was only a single morning before the summer holidays, and that morning was occupied with the prize-giving. The school assembled at ten o'clock with a shadowy hope that this prize-day would be more exciting than the general run of prize-days, but they were disappointed. The function passed off without sensation. The headmaster did not denounce the school in an impassioned speech from the dais. He did not refer to the events of the previous evening. At the same time, his demeanour was far from jovial. It lacked that rollicking bonhomie which we like to see in headmasters on prize-day. It was evident to the most casual observer that the affair was not closed. The school would have to pay the bill sooner or later. But eight weeks would elapse before the day of reckoning, which was a comforting thought.

The last prize was handed over to its rightful owner. The last and dullest vote of thanks had been proposed by the last and dullest member of the board of governors. The Bishop of Rumtifoo (who had been selected this year to distribute the prizes) had worked off his seventy minutes' speech (inaudible, of course, as usual), and was feeling much easier. The term had been formally declared at an end, and those members of the school corps who were going to camp were beginning to assemble in front of the buildings.

"I wonder why it always takes about three hours to get us off to the station," said Jimmy Silver. "I've been to camp two years now, and there's always been this rotting about in the grounds before we start. Nobody's likely to turn up to inspect us for the next hour or so. If any gent cares to put in a modest ginger-beer at the shop, I'm with him."

"I don't see why we shouldn't," said Kennedy. He had seen Fenn go into the shop, and wished to talk to him. He had not seen him after the concert, and he thought it would be interesting to know how Kay had taken it, and what his comments had been on meeting Fenn in the house that night.

Fenn had not much to say.

"He was rather worried," he said, grinning as if the recollection of the interview amused him. "But he couldn't do anything. Of course, there'll be a row next term, but it can't be helped."

"If I were you," said Silver, "I should point out to them that you'd a perfect right to play what you liked for an encore. How were you to know the gallery would go off like that? You aren't responsible for them. Hullo, there's that bugle. Things seem to be on the move. We must go."

"So long," said Fenn.

"Goodbye. Mind you come off against Middlesex."

Kennedy stayed for a moment.

"Has the Old Man said anything to you yet?" he asked.

"Not yet. He'll do that next term. It'll be something to look forward to."

Kennedy hurried off to take his place in the ranks.

Getting to camp at the end of the summer term is always a nuisance. Aldershot seems a long way from everywhere, and the trains take their time over the journey. Then, again, the heat always happens to be particularly oppressive on that day. Snow may have fallen on the day before, but directly one sets out for camp, the thermometer goes up into three figures. The Eckleton contingent marched into the lines damp and very thirsty.

Most of the other schools were already on the spot, and looked as if they had been spending the last few years there. There was nothing particular going on when the Eckleton warriors arrived, and everybody was lounging about in khaki and shirt-sleeves, looking exasperatingly cool. The only consolation which buoyed up the spirits of Eckleton was the reflection that in a short space of time, when the important-looking gentleman in uniform who had come to meet them had said all he wanted to say on the subject of rules and regulations, they would be like that too. Happy thought! If the man

27

bucked up and cut short the peroration, there would be time for a bathe in Cove Reservoir. Those of the corps who had been to camp in previous years felt quite limp with the joy of the thought. Why couldn't he get through with it, and give a fellow a chance of getting cool again?

The gist of the oration was apparently that the Eckleton cadets were to consider themselves not only as soldiers—and as such subject to military discipline, and the rules for the conduct of troops quartered in the Aldershot district—but also as members of a public school. In short, that if they misbehaved themselves they would get cells, and a hundred lines in the same breath, as it were.

The corps knew all this ages ago. The man seemed to think he was telling them something fresh. They began positively to dislike him after a while.

He finished at last. Eckleton marched off wearily, but in style, to its lines.

"Dis-miss!"

They did.

"And about time, too," said Jimmy Silver. "I wish they would tie that man up, or something. He's one of the worst bores I know. He may be full of bright conversation in private life, but in public he will talk about his beastly military regulations. You can't stop him. It's a perfect mania with him. Now, I believe—that's to say, I have a sort of dim idea—that there's a place round about here called a canteen. I seem to remember such a thing vaguely. We might go and look for it."

Kennedy made no objection.

This was his first appearance at camp. Jimmy Silver, on the other hand, was a veteran. He had been there twice before, and meant to go again. He had a peculiar and extensive knowledge of the ins and outs of the place. Kennedy was quite willing to take him as his guide. He was full of information. Kennedy was surprised to see what a number of men from the other schools he seemed to know. In the canteen there were, amongst others, a Carthusian, two Tonbridge men, and a Haileyburian. They all greeted Silver with the warmth of old friends.

28

"You get to know a lot of fellows in camp," explained Jimmy, as they strolled back to the Eckleton lines. "That's the best of the place. Camp's the best place on earth, if only you have decent weather. See that chap over there? He came here last year. He'd never been before, and one of the things he didn't know was that Cove Reservoir's only about three feet deep round the sides. He took a running dive, and almost buried himself in the mud. It's about two feet deep. He told me afterwards he swallowed pounds of it. Rather bad luck. Somebody ought to have told him. You can't do much diving here."

"Glad you mentioned it," said Kennedy. "I should have dived myself if you hadn't."

Many other curious and diverting facts did the expert drag from the bonded warehouse of his knowledge. Nothing changes at camp. Once get to know the ropes, and you know them for all time.

"The one thing I bar," he said, "is having to get up at half-past five. And one day in the week, when there's a divisional field-day, it's half-past four. It's hardly worth while going to sleep at all. Still, it isn't so bad as it used to be. The first year I came to camp we used to have to do a three hours' field-day before brekker. We used to have coffee before it, and nothing else till it was over. By Jove, you felt you'd had enough of it before you got back. This is Laffan's Plain. The worst of Laffan's Plain is that you get to know it too well. You get jolly sick of always starting on field-days from the same place, and marching across the same bit of ground. Still, I suppose they can't alter the scenery for our benefit. See that man there? He won the sabres at Aldershot last year. That chap with him is in the Clifton footer team."

When a school corps goes to camp, it lives in a number of tents, and, as a rule, each house collects in a tent of its own. Blackburn's had a tent, and further down the line Kay's had assembled. The Kay contingent were under Wayburn, a good sort, as far as he himself was concerned, but too weak to handle a mob like Kay's. Wayburn was not coming back after the holidays, a fact which perhaps still further weakened his hold on the Kayites. They had nothing to fear from him next term.

Kay's was represented at camp by a dozen or so of its members, of whom young Billy Silver alone had any pretensions to the esteem of his fellow man. Kay's was the rowdiest house in the school, and the

29

cream of its rowdy members had come to camp. There was Walton, for one, a perfect specimen of the public school man at his worst. There was Mortimer, another of Kay's gems. Perry, again, and Callingham, and the rest. A pleasant gang, fit for anything, if it could be done in safety.

Kennedy observed them, and—the spectacle starting a train of thought—asked Jimmy Silver, as they went into their tent just before lights-out, if there was much ragging in camp.

"Not very much," said the expert. "Chaps are generally too done up at the end of the day to want to do anything except sleep. Still, I've known cases. You sometimes get one tent mobbing another. They loose the ropes, you know. Low trick, I think. It isn't often done, and it gets dropped on like bricks when it's found out. But why? Do you feel as if you wanted to do it?"

"It only occurred to me that we've got a lively gang from Kay's here. I was wondering if they'd get any chances of ragging, or if they'd have to lie low."

"I'd forgotten Kay's for the moment. Now you mention it, they are rather a crew. But I shouldn't think they'd find it worth while to rot about here. It isn't as if they were on their native heath. People have a prejudice against having their tent-ropes loosed, and they'd get beans if they did anything in that line. I remember once there was a tent which made itself objectionable, and it got raided in the night by a sort of vigilance committee from the other schools, and the chaps in it got the dickens of a time. None of them ever came to camp again. I hope Kay's'll try and behave decently. It'll be an effort for them; but I hope they'll make it. It would be an awful nuisance if young Billy made an ass of himself in any way. He loves making an ass of himself. It's a sort of hobby of his."

As if to support the statement, a sudden volley of subdued shouts came from the other end of the Eckleton lines.

"Go it, Wren!"

"Stick to it, Silver!"

"Wren!"

"Silver!"

"S-s-h!"

Silence, followed almost immediately by a gruff voice inquiring with simple directness what the dickens all this noise was about.

"Hullo!" said Kennedy. "Did you hear that? I wonder what's been up? Your brother was in it, whatever it was."

"Of course," said Jimmy Silver, "he would be. We can't find out about it now, though. I'll ask him tomorrow, if I remember. I shan't remember, of course. Good night."

"Good night."

Half an hour later, Kennedy, who had been ruminating over the incident in his usual painstaking way, reopened the debate.

"Who's Wren?" he asked.

"Wha'?" murmured Silver, sleepily.

"Who's Wren?" repeated Kennedy.

"I d'know.... Oh.... Li'l' beast.... Kay's.... Red hair.... G'-ni'."

And sleep reigned in Blackburn's tent.

31

THE RAID ON THE GUARD-TENT

Wren and Billy Silver had fallen out over a question of space. It was Silver's opinion that Wren's nest ought to have been built a foot or two further to the left. He stated baldly that he had not room to breathe, and requested the red-headed one to ease off a point or so in the direction of his next-door neighbour. Wren had refused, and, after a few moments' chatty conversation, smote William earnestly in the wind. Trouble had begun upon the instant. It had ceased almost as rapidly owing to interruptions from without, but the truce had been merely temporary. They continued the argument outside the tent at five-thirty the next morning, after the reveille had sounded, amidst shouts of approval from various shivering mortals who were tubbing preparatory to embarking on the labours of the day.

A brisk first round had just come to a conclusion when Walton lounged out of the tent, yawning.

Walton proceeded to separate the combatants. After which he rebuked Billy Silver with a swagger-stick. Wren's share in the business he overlooked. He was by way of being a patron of Wren's, and he disliked Billy Silver, partly for his own sake and partly because he hated his brother, with whom he had come into contact once or twice during his career at Eckleton, always with unsatisfactory results.

So Walton dropped on to Billy Silver, and Wren continued his toilet rejoicing.

Camp was beginning the strenuous life now. Tent after tent emptied itself of its occupants, who stretched themselves vigorously, and proceeded towards the tubbing-ground, where there were tin baths for those who cared to wait until the same were vacant, and a good, honest pump for those who did not. Then there was that unpopular job, the piling of one's bedding outside the tent, and the rolling up of the tent curtains. But these unpleasant duties came to an end at last, and signs of breakfast began to appear.

Breakfast gave Kennedy his first insight into life in camp. He happened to be tent-orderly that day, and it therefore fell to his lot to join the orderlies from the other tents in their search for the Eckleton rations. He returned with a cargo of bread (obtained from the quartermaster), and, later, with a great tin of meat, which the cook-house had supplied, and felt that this was life. Hitherto breakfast had been to him a thing of white cloths, tables, and food that appeared from nowhere. This was the first time he had ever tracked his food to its source, so to speak, and brought it back with him. After breakfast, when he was informed that, as tent-orderly for the day, it was his business to wash up, he began to feel as if he were on a desert island. He had never quite realised before what washing-up implied, and he was conscious of a feeling of respect for the servants at Blackburn's, who did it every day as a matter of course, without complaint. He had had no idea before this of the intense stickiness of a jammy plate.

One day at camp is much like another. The schools opened the day with parade drill at about eight o'clock, and, after an instruction series of "changing direction half-left in column of double companies", and other pleasant movements of a similar nature, adjourned for lunch. Lunch was much like breakfast, except that the supply of jam was cut off. The people who arrange these things— probably the War Office, or Mr Brodrick, or someone—have come to the conclusion that two pots of jam per tent are sufficient for breakfast and lunch. The unwary devour theirs recklessly at the earlier meal, and have to go jamless until tea at six o'clock, when another pot is served out.

The afternoon at camp is perfect or otherwise, according to whether there is a four o'clock field-day or not. If there is, there are more manoeuvrings until tea-time, and the time is spent profitably, but not so pleasantly as it might be. If there is no field-day, you can take your time about your bathe in Cove Reservoir. And a really satisfactory bathe on a hot day should last at least three hours. Kennedy and Jimmy Silver strolled off in the direction of the Reservoir as soon as they felt that they had got over the effects of the beef, potatoes, and ginger-beer which a generous commissariat had doled out to them for lunch. It was a glorious day, and bathing was the only thing to do for the next hour or so. Stump-cricket, that fascinating sport much indulged in in camp, would not be at its best until the sun had cooled off a little.

After a pleasant half hour in the mud and water of the Reservoir, they lay on the bank and watched the rest of the schools take their afternoon dip. Kennedy had laid in a supply of provisions from the stall which stood at the camp end of the water. Neither of them felt inclined to move.

"This is decent," said Kennedy, wriggling into a more comfortable position in the long grass. "Hullo!"

"What's up?" inquired Jimmy Silver, lazily.

He was almost asleep.

"Look at those idiots. They're certain to get spotted."

Jimmy Silver tilted his hat off his face, and sat up.

"What's the matter? Which idiot?"

Kennedy pointed to a bush on their right. Walton and Perry were seated beside it. Both were smoking.

"Oh, that's all right," said Silver. "Masters never come to Cove Reservoir. It's a sort of unwritten law. They're rotters to smoke, all the same. Certain to get spotted some day.... Not worth it.... Spoils lungs.... Beastly bad ... training."

He dozed off. The sun was warm, and the grass very soft and comfortable. Kennedy turned his gaze to the Reservoir again. It was no business of his what Walton and Perry did.

Walton and Perry were discussing ways and means. The conversation changed as they saw Kennedy glance at them. They were the sort of persons who feel a vague sense of injury when anybody looks at them, perhaps because they feel that those whose attention is attracted to them must say something to their discredit when they begin to talk about them.

"There's that beast Kennedy," said Walton. "I can't stick that man. He's always hanging round the house. What he comes for, I can't make out."

"Pal of Fenn's," suggested Perry.

"He hangs on to Fenn. I bet Fenn bars him really."

Perry doubted this in his innermost thoughts, but it was not worth while to say so.

"Those Blackburn chaps," continued Walton, reverting to another grievance, "will stick on no end of side next term about that cup. They wouldn't have had a look in if Kay hadn't given Fenn that extra. Kay ought to be kicked. I'm hanged if I'm going to care what I do next term. Somebody ought to do something to take it out of Kay for getting his own house licked like that."

Walton spoke as if the line of conduct he had mapped out for himself would be a complete reversal of his customary mode of life. As a matter of fact, he had never been in the habit of caring very much what he did.

Walton's last remarks brought the conversation back to where it had been before the mention of Kennedy switched it off on to new lines. Perry had been complaining that he thought camp a fraud, that it was all drilling and getting up at unearthly hours. He reminded Walton that he had only come on the strength of the latter's statement that it would be a rag. Where did the rag come in? That was what Perry wanted to know.

"When it's not a ghastly sweat," he concluded, "it's slow. Like it is now. Can't we do something for a change?"

"As a matter of fact," said Walton, "nearly all the best rags are played out. A chap at a crammer's told me last holidays that when he was at camp he and some other fellows loosed the ropes of the guard-tent. He said it was grand sport."

Perry sat up.

"That's the thing," he said, excitedly. "Let's do that. Why not?"

"It's beastly risky," objected Walton.

"What's that matter? They can't do anything, even if they spot us."

"That's all you know. We should get beans."

"Still, it's worth risking. It would be the biggest rag going. Did the chap tell you how they did it?"

"Yes," said Walton, becoming animated as he recalled the stirring tale, "they bagged the sentry. Chucked a cloth or something over his head, you know. Then they shoved him into the ditch, and one of them sat on him while the others loosed the ropes. It took the chaps inside no end of a time getting out."

"That's the thing. We'll do it. We only need one other chap. Leveson would come if we asked him. Let's get back to the lines. It's almost tea-time. Tell him after tea."

Leveson proved agreeable. Indeed, he jumped at it. His life, his attitude suggested, had been a hollow mockery until he heard the plan, but now he could begin to enjoy himself once more.

The lights-out bugle sounded at ten o'clock; the last post at ten-thirty. At a quarter to twelve the three adventurers, who had been keeping themselves awake by the exercise of great pains, satisfied themselves that the other occupants of the tent were asleep, and stole out.

It was an excellent night for their purpose. There was no moon, and the stars were hidden by clouds.

They crept silently towards the guard-tent. A dim figure loomed out of the blackness. They noted with satisfaction, as it approached, that it was small. Sentries at the public-school camp vary in physique. They felt that it was lucky that the task of sentry-go had not fallen that night to some muscular forward from one of the school fifteens, or worse still, to a boxing expert who had figured in the Aldershot competition at Easter. The present sentry would be an easy victim.

They waited for him to arrive.

A moment later Private Jones, of St Asterisk's—for it was he—turning to resume his beat, found himself tackled from behind. Two moments later he was reclining in the ditch. He would have challenged his adversary, but, unfortunately, that individual happened to be seated on his face.

He struggled, but to no purpose.

He was still struggling when a muffled roar of indignation from the direction of the guard-tent broke the stillness of the summer night. The roar swelled into a crescendo. What seemed like echoes came from other quarters out of the darkness. The camp was waking.

The noise from the guard-tent waxed louder.

The unknown marauder rose from his seat on Private Jones, and vanished.

Private Jones also rose. He climbed out of the ditch, shook himself, looked round for his assailant, and, not finding him, hurried to the guard-tent to see what was happening.

36

VII

A CLUE

The guard-tent had disappeared.

Private Jones' bewildered eye, rolling in a fine frenzy from heaven to earth, and from earth to heaven, in search of the missing edifice, found it at last in a tangled heap upon the ground. It was too dark to see anything distinctly, but he perceived that the canvas was rising and falling spasmodically like a stage sea, and for a similar reason—because there were human beings imprisoned beneath it.

By this time the whole camp was up and doing. Figures in deshabille, dashing the last vestiges of sleep away with their knuckles, trooped on to the scene in twos and threes, full of inquiry and trenchant sarcasm.

"What are you men playing at? What's all the row about? Can't you finish that game of footer some other time, when we aren't trying to get to sleep? What on earth's up?"

Then the voice of one having authority.

"What's the matter? What are you doing?"

It was perfectly obvious what the guard was doing. It was trying to get out from underneath the fallen tent. Private Jones explained this with some warmth.

"Somebody jumped at me and sat on my head in the ditch. I couldn't get up. And then some blackguard cut the ropes of the guard-tent. I couldn't see who it was. He cut off directly the tent went down."

Private Jones further expressed a wish that he could find the chap. When he did, there would, he hinted, be trouble in the old homestead.

The tent was beginning to disgorge its prisoners.

"Guard, turn out!" said a facetious voice from the darkness.

37

The camp was divided into two schools of thought. Those who were watching the guard struggle out thought the episode funny. The guard did not. It was pathetic to hear them on the subject of their mysterious assailants. Matters quieted down rapidly after the tent had been set up again. The spectators were driven back to their lines by their officers. The guard turned in again to try and restore their shattered nerves with sleep until their time for sentry-go came round. Private Jones picked up his rifle and resumed his beat. The affair was at an end as far as that night was concerned.

Next morning, as might be expected, nothing else was talked about. Conversation at breakfast was confined to the topic. No halfpenny paper, however many times its circulation might exceed that of any penny morning paper, ever propounded so fascinating and puzzling a breakfast-table problem. It was the utter impossibility of detecting the culprits that appealed to the schools. They had swooped down like hawks out of the night, and disappeared like eels into mud, leaving no traces.

Jimmy Silver, of course, had no doubts.

"It was those Kay's men," he said. "What does it matter about evidence? You've only got to look at 'em. That's all the evidence you want. The only thing that makes it at all puzzling is that they did nothing worse. You'd naturally expect them to slay the sentry, at any rate."

But the rest of the camp, lacking that intimate knowledge of the Kayite which he possessed, did not turn the eye of suspicion towards the Eckleton lines. The affair remained a mystery. Kennedy, who never gave up a problem when everybody else did, continued to revolve the mystery in his mind.

"I shouldn't wonder," he said to Silver, two days later, "if you were right."

Silver, who had not made any remark for the last five minutes, with the exception of abusive comments on the toughness of the meat which he was trying to carve with a blunt knife for the tent, asked for an explanation. "I mean about that row the other night."

"What row?"

"That guard-tent business."

"Oh, that! I'd forgotten. Why don't you move with the times? You're always thinking of something that's been dead and buried for years."

"You remember you said you thought it was those Kay's chaps who did it. I've been thinking it over, and I believe you're right. You see, it was probably somebody who'd been to camp before, or he wouldn't have known that dodge of loosing the ropes."

"I don't see why. Seems to me it's the sort of idea that might have occurred to anybody. You don't want to study the thing particularly deeply to know that the best way of making a tent collapse is to loose the ropes. Of course it was Kay's lot who did it. But I don't see how you're going to have them simply because one or two of them have been here before."

"No, I suppose not," said Kennedy.

After tea the other occupants of the tent went out of the lines to play stump-cricket. Silver was in the middle of a story in one of the magazines, so did not accompany them. Kennedy cried off on the plea of slackness.

"I say," he said, when they were alone.

"Hullo," said Silver, finishing his story, and putting down the magazine. "What do you say to going after those chaps? I thought that story was going to be a long one that would take half an hour to get through. But it collapsed. Like that guard-tent."

"About that tent business," said Kennedy. "Of course that was all rot what I was saying just now. I suddenly remembered that I didn't particularly want anybody but you to hear what I was going to say, so I had to invent any rot that I could think of."

"But now," said Jimmy Silver, sinking his voice to a melodramatic whisper, "the villagers have left us to continue their revels on the green, our wicked uncle has gone to London, his sinister retainer, Jasper Murgleshaw, is washing his hands in the scullery sink, and— we are alone!"

"Don't be an ass," pleaded Kennedy.

"Tell me your dreadful tale. Conceal nothing. Spare me not. In fact, say on."

"I've had a talk with the chap who was sentry that night," began Kennedy.

"Astounding revelations by our special correspondent," murmured Silver.

"You might listen."

"I am listening. Why don't you begin? All this hesitation strikes me as suspicious. Get on with your shady story."

"You remember the sentry was upset—"

"Very upset."

"Somebody collared him from behind, and upset him into the ditch. They went in together, and the other man sat on his head."

"A touching picture. Proceed, friend."

"They rolled about a bit, and this sentry chap swears he scratched the man. It was just after that that the man sat on his head. Jones says he was a big chap, strong and heavy."

"He was in a position to judge, anyhow."

"Of course, he didn't mean to scratch him. He was rather keen on having that understood. But his fingers came up against the fellow's cheek as he was falling. So you see we've only got to look for a man with a scratch on his cheek. It was the right cheek, Jones was almost certain. I don't see what you're laughing at."

"I wish you wouldn't spring these good things of yours on me suddenly," gurgled Jimmy Silver, rolling about the wooden floor of the tent. "You ought to give a chap some warning. Look here," he added, imperatively, "swear you'll take me with you when you go on your tour through camp examining everybody's right cheek to see if it's got a scratch on it."

Kennedy began to feel the glow and pride of the successful sleuth-hound leaking out of him. This aspect of the case had not occurred to him. The fact that the sentry had scratched his assailant's right cheek, added to the other indubitable fact that Walton, of Kay's, was even now walking abroad with a scratch on his right cheek, had seemed to him conclusive. He had forgotten that there might be

40

others. Still, it was worth while just to question him. He questioned him at Cove Reservoir next day.

"Hullo, Walton," he said, with a friendly carelessness which would not have deceived a prattling infant, "nasty scratch you've got on your cheek. How did you get it?"

"Perry did it when we were ragging a few days ago," replied Walton, eyeing him distrustfully.

"Oh," said Kennedy.

"Silly fool," said Walton.

"Talking about me?" inquired Kennedy politely.

"No," replied Walton, with the suavity of a Chesterfield, "Perry."

They parted, Kennedy with the idea that Walton was his man still more deeply rooted, Walton with an uncomfortable feeling that Kennedy knew too much, and that, though he had undoubtedly scored off him for the moment, a time (as Jimmy Silver was fond of observing with a satanic laugh) would come, and then—!

He felt that it behoved him to be wary.

VIII

A NIGHT ADVENTURE—THE DETHRONEMENT OF FENN

One of the things which make life on this planet more or less agreeable is the speed with which alarums, excursions, excitement, and rows generally, blow over. A nine-days' wonder has to be a big business to last out its full time nowadays. As a rule the third day sees the end of it, and the public rushes whooping after some other hare that has been started for its benefit. The guard-tent row, as far as the bulk of camp was concerned, lasted exactly two days; at the end of which period it was generally agreed that all that could be said on the subject had been said, and that it was now a back number. Nobody, except possibly the authorities, wanted to find out the authors of the raid, and even Private Jones had ceased to talk about it—this owing to the unsympathetic attitude of his tent.

"Jones," the corporal had observed, as the ex-sentry's narrative of his misfortunes reached a finish for the third time since reveille that morning, "if you can't manage to switch off that infernal chestnut of yours, I'll make you wash up all day and sit on your head all night."

So Jones had withdrawn his yarn from circulation. Kennedy's interest in detective work waned after his interview with Walton. He was quite sure that Walton had been one of the band, but it was not his business to find out; even had he found out, he would have done nothing. It was more for his own private satisfaction than for the furtherance of justice that he wished to track the offenders down. But he did not look on the affair, as Jimmy Silver did, as rather sporting; he had a tender feeling for the good name of the school, and he felt that it was not likely to make Eckleton popular with the other schools that went to camp if they got the reputation of practical jokers. Practical jokers are seldom popular until they have been dead a hundred years or so.

As for Walton and his colleagues, to complete the list of those who were interested in this matter of the midnight raid, they lay remarkably low after their successful foray. They imagined that

42

Kennedy was spying on their every movement. In which they were quite wrong, for Kennedy was doing nothing of the kind. Camp does not allow a great deal of leisure for the minding of other people's businesses. But this reflection did not occur to Walton, and he regarded Kennedy, whenever chance or his duties brought him into the neighbourhood of that worthy's tent, with a suspicion which increased whenever the latter looked at him.

On the night before camp broke up, a second incident of a sensational kind occurred, which, but for the fact that they never heard of it, would have given the schools a good deal to talk about. It happened that Kennedy was on sentry-go that night. The manner of sentry-go is thus. At seven in the evening the guard falls in, and patrols the fringe of the camp in relays till seven in the morning. A guard consists of a sergeant, a corporal, and ten men. They are on duty for two hours at a time, with intervals of four hours between each spell, in which intervals they sleep the sleep of tired men in the guard-tent, unless, as happened on the occasion previously described, some miscreant takes it upon himself to loose the ropes. The ground to be patrolled by the sentries is divided into three parts, each of which is entrusted to one man.

Kennedy was one of the ten privates, and his first spell of sentry-go began at eleven o'clock.

On this night there was no moon. It was as black as pitch. It is always unpleasant to be on sentry-go on such a night. The mind wanders, in spite of all effort to check it, through a long series of all the ghastly stories one has ever read. There is one in particular of Conan Doyle's about a mummy that came to life and chased people on lonely roads—but enough! However courageous one may be, it is difficult not to speculate on the possible horrors which may spring out on one from the darkness. That feeling that there is somebody— or something—just behind one can only be experienced in all its force by a sentry on an inky night at camp. And the thought that, of all the hundreds there, he and two others are the only ones awake, puts a sort of finishing touch to the unpleasantness of the situation.

Kennedy was not a particularly imaginative youth, but he looked forward with no little eagerness to the time when he should be relieved. It would be a relief in two senses of the word. His beat included that side of the camp which faces the road to Aldershot. Between camp and this road is a ditch and a wood. After he had been on duty for an hour this wood began to suggest a variety of

43

possibilities, all grim. The ditch, too, was not without associations. It was into this that Private Jones had been hurled on a certain memorable occasion. Such a thing was not likely to happen again in the same week, and, even if it did, Kennedy flattered himself that he would have more to say in the matter than Private Jones had had; but nevertheless he kept a careful eye in that direction whenever his beat took him along the ditch.

It was about half-past twelve, and he had entered upon the last section of his two hours, when Kennedy distinctly heard footsteps in the wood. He had heard so many mysterious sounds since his patrol began at eleven o'clock that at first he was inclined to attribute this to imagination. But a crackle of dead branches and the sound of soft breathing convinced him that this was the real thing for once, and that, as a sentry of the Public Schools' Camp on duty, it behoved him to challenge the unknown.

He stopped and waited, peering into the darkness in a futile endeavour to catch a glimpse of his man. But the night was too black for the keenest eye to penetrate it. A slight thud put him on the right track. It showed him two things; first, that the unknown had dropped into the ditch, and, secondly, that he was a camp man returning to his tent after an illegal prowl about the town at lights-out. Nobody save one belonging to the camp would have cause to cross the ditch.

Besides, the man walked warily, as one not ignorant of the danger of sentries. The unknown had crawled out of the ditch now. As luck would have it he had chosen a spot immediately opposite to where Kennedy stood. Now that he was nearer Kennedy could see the vague outline of him.

"Who goes there?" he said.

From an instinctive regard for the other's feelings he did not shout the question in the regulation manner. He knew how he would feel himself if he were out of camp at half-past twelve, and the voice of the sentry were to rip suddenly through the silence fortissimo.

As it was, his question was quite loud enough to electrify the person to whom it was addressed. The unknown started so violently that he nearly leapt into the air. Kennedy was barely two yards from him when he spoke.

The next moment this fact was brought home to him in a very

practical manner. The unknown, sighting the sentry, perhaps more clearly against the dim whiteness of the tents than Kennedy could sight him against the dark wood, dashed in with a rapidity which showed that he knew something of the art of boxing. Kennedy dropped his rifle and flung up his arm. He was altogether too late. A sudden blaze of light, and he was on the ground, sick and dizzy, a feeling he had often experienced before in a slighter degree, when sparring in the Eckleton gymnasium with the boxing instructor.

The immediate effect of a flush hit in the regions about the jaw is to make the victim lose for the moment all interest in life. Kennedy lay where he had fallen for nearly half a minute before he fully realised what it was that had happened to him. When he did realise the situation, he leapt to his feet, feeling sick and shaky, and staggered about in all directions in a manner which suggested that he fancied his assailant would be waiting politely until he had recovered. As was only natural, that wily person had vanished, and was by this time doing a quick change into garments of the night. Kennedy had the satisfaction of knowing—for what it was worth—that his adversary was in one of those tents, but to place him with any greater accuracy was impossible.

So he gave up the search, found his rifle, and resumed his patrol. And at one o'clock his successor relieved him.

On the following day camp broke up.

Kennedy always enjoyed going home, but, as he travelled back to Eckleton on the last day of these summer holidays, he could not help feeling that there was a great deal to be said for term. He felt particularly cheerful. He had the carriage to himself, and he had also plenty to read and eat. The train was travelling at forty miles an hour. And there were all the pleasures of a first night after the holidays to look forward to, when you dashed from one friend's study to another's, comparing notes, and explaining—five or six of you at a time—what a good time you had had in the holidays. This was always a pleasant ceremony at Blackburn's, where all the prefects were intimate friends, and all good sorts, without that liberal admixture of weeds, worms, and outsiders which marred the list of prefects in most of the other houses. Such as Kay's! Kennedy could not restrain a momentary gloating as he contrasted the state of affairs in Blackburn's with what existed at Kay's. Then this feeling was merged in one of pity for Fenn's hard case. How he must hate the beginning of term, thought Kennedy.

45

All the well-known stations were flashing by now. In a few minutes he would be at the junction, and in another half-hour back at Blackburn's. He began to collect his baggage from the rack.

Nobody he knew was at the junction. This was the late train that he had come down by. Most of the school had returned earlier in the afternoon.

He reached Blackburn's at eight o'clock, and went up to his study to unpack. This was always his first act on coming back to school. He liked to start the term with all his books in their shelves, and all his pictures and photographs in their proper places on the first day. Some of the studies looked like lumber-rooms till near the end of the first week.

He had filled the shelves, and was arranging the artistic decorations, when Jimmy Silver came in. Kennedy had been surprised that he had not met him downstairs, but the matron had answered his inquiry with the statement that he was talking to Mr Blackburn in the other part of the house.

"When did you arrive?" asked Silver, after the conclusion of the first outbreak of holiday talk.

"I've only just come."

"Seen Blackburn yet?"

"No. I was thinking of going up after I had got this place done properly."

Jimmy Silver ran his eye over the room.

"I haven't started mine yet," he said. "You're such an energetic man. Now, are all those books in their proper places?"

"Yes," said Kennedy.

"Sure?"

"Yes."

"How about the pictures? Got them up?"

"All but this lot here. Shan't be a second. There you are. How's that for effect?"

46

"Not bad. Got all your photographs in their places?"

"Yes."

"Then," said Jimmy Silver, calmly, "you'd better start now to pack them all up again. And why, my son? Because you are no longer a Blackburnite. That's what."

Kennedy stared.

"I've just had the whole yarn from Blackburn," continued Jimmy Silver. "Our dear old pal, Mr Kay, wanting somebody in his house capable of keeping order, by way of a change, has gone to the Old Man and borrowed you. So you're head of Kay's now. There's an honour for you."

IX

THE SENSATIONS OF AN EXILE

"What" shouted Kennedy.

He sprang to his feet as if he had had an electric shock.

Jimmy Silver, having satisfied his passion for the dramatic by the abruptness with which he had exploded his mine, now felt himself at liberty to be sympathetic.

"It's quite true," he said. "And that's just how I felt when Blackburn told me. Blackburn's as sick as anything. Naturally he doesn't see the point of handing you over to Kay. But the Old Man insisted, so he caved in. He wanted to see you as soon as you arrived. You'd better go now. I'll finish your packing."

This was noble of Jimmy, for of all the duties of life he loathed packing most.

"Thanks awfully," said Kennedy, "but don't you bother. I'll do it when I get back. But what's it all about? What made Kay want a man? Why won't Fenn do? And why me?"

"Well, it's easy to see why they chose you. They reflected that you'd had the advantage of being in Blackburn's with me, and seeing how a house really should be run. Kay wants a head for his house. Off he goes to the Old Man. 'Look here,' he says, 'I want somebody shunted into my happy home, or it'll bust up. And it's no good trying to put me off with an inferior article, because I won't have it. It must be somebody who's been trained from youth up by Silver.' 'Then,' says the Old Man, reflectively, 'you can't do better than take Kennedy. I happen to know that Silver has spent years in showing him the straight and narrow path. You take Kennedy.' 'All right,' says Kay; 'I always thought Kennedy a bit of an ass myself, but if he's studied under Silver he ought to know how to manage a house. I'll take him. Advise our Mr Blackburn to that effect, and ask him to deliver the goods at his earliest convenience. Adoo, mess-mate, adoo!' And there you are—that's how it was."

"But what's wrong with Fenn?"

"My dear chap! Remember last term. Didn't Fenn have a regular scrap with Kay, and get shoved into extra for it? And didn't he wreck the concert in the most sportsmanlike way with that encore of his? Think the Old Man is going to take that grinning? Not much! Fenn made a ripping fifty against Kent in the holidays—I saw him do it—but they don't count that. It's a wonder they didn't ask him to leave. Of course, I think it's jolly rough on Fenn, but I don't see that you can blame them. Not the Old Man, at any rate. He couldn't do anything else. It's all Kay's fault that all this has happened, of course. I'm awfully sorry for you having to go into that beastly hole, but from Kay's point of view it's a jolly sound move. You may reform the place."

"I doubt it."

"So do I—very much. I didn't say you would—I said you might. I wonder if Kay means to give you a free hand. It all depends on that."

"Yes. If he's going to interfere with me as he used to with Fenn, he'll want to bring in another head to improve on me."

"Rather a good idea, that," said Jimmy Silver, laughing, as he always did when any humorous possibilities suggested themselves to him. "If he brings in somebody to improve on you, and then somebody else to improve on him, and then another chap to improve on him, he ought to have a decent house in half-a-dozen years or so."

"The worst of it is," said Kennedy, "that I've got to go to Kay's as a sort of rival to Fenn. I shouldn't mind so much if it wasn't for that. I wonder how he'll take it! Do you think he knows about it yet? He didn't enjoy being head, but that's no reason why he shouldn't cut up rough at being shoved back to second prefect. It's a beastly situation."

"Beastly," agreed Jimmy Silver. "Look here," he added, after a pause, "there's no reason, you know, why this should make any difference. To us, I mean. What I mean to say is, I don't see why we shouldn't see each other just as often, and so on, simply because you are in another house, and all that sort of thing. You know what I mean."

He spoke shamefacedly, as was his habit whenever he was serious. He liked Kennedy better than anyone he knew, and hated to show his feelings. Anything remotely connected with sentiment made him uncomfortable.

"Of course," said Kennedy, awkwardly.

"You'll want a refuge," said Silver, in his normal manner, "now that you're going to see wild life in Kay's. Don't forget that I'm always at home in my study in the afternoons—admission on presentation of a visiting-card."

"All right," said Kennedy, "I'll remember. I suppose I'd better go and see Blackburn now."

Mr Blackburn was in his study. He was obviously disgusted and irritated by what had happened. Loyalty to the headmaster, and an appreciation of his position as a member of the staff led him to try and conceal his feelings as much as possible in his interview with Kennedy, but the latter understood as plainly as if his house-master had burst into a flow of abuse and complaint. There had always been an excellent understanding—indeed, a friendship—between Kennedy and Mr Blackburn, and the master was just as sorry to lose his second prefect as the latter was to go.

"Well, Kennedy," he said, pleasantly. "I hope you had a good time in the holidays. I suppose Silver has told you the melancholy news—that you are to desert us this term? It is a great pity. We shall all be very sorry to lose you. I don't look forward to seeing you bowl us all out in the house-matches next summer," he added, with a smile, "though we shall expect a few full-pitches to leg, for the sake of old times."

He meant well, but the picture he conjured up almost made Kennedy break down. Nothing up to the present had made him realise the completeness of his exile so keenly as this remark of Mr Blackburn's about his bowling against the side for which he had taken so many wickets in the past. It was a painful thought.

"I am afraid you won't have quite such a pleasant time in Mr Kay's as you have had here," resumed the house-master. "Of course, I know that, strictly speaking, I ought not to talk like this about another master's house; but you can scarcely be unaware of the reasons that have led to this change. You must know that you are being sent to pull Mr Kay's house together. This is strictly between ourselves, of course. I think you have a difficult task before you, but

I don't fancy that you will find it too much for you. And mind you come here as often as you please. I am sure Silver and the others will be glad to see you. Goodbye, Kennedy. I think you ought to be getting across now to Mr Kay's. I told him that you would be there before half-past nine. Good night."

"Good night, sir," said Kennedy.

He wandered out into the house dining-room. Somehow, though Kay's was only next door, he could not get rid of the feeling that he was about to start on a long journey, and would never see his old house again. And in a sense this was so. He would probably visit Blackburn's tomorrow afternoon, but it would not be the same. Jimmy Silver would greet him like a brother, and he would brew in the same study in which he had always brewed, and sit in the same chair; but it would not be the same. He would be an outsider, a visitor, a stranger within the gates, and—worst of all—a Kayite. Nothing could alter that.

The walk of the dining-room were covered with photographs of the house cricket and football teams for the last fifteen years. Looking at them, he felt more than ever how entirely his school life had been bound up in his house. From his first day at Eckleton he had been taught the simple creed of the Blackburnite, that Eckleton was the finest school in the three kingdoms, and that Blackburn's was the finest house in the finest school.

Under the gas-bracket by the door hung the first photograph in which he appeared, the cricket team of four years ago. He had just got the last place in front of Challis on the strength of a tremendous catch for the house second in a scratch game two days before the house-matches began. It had been a glaring fluke, but it had impressed Denny, the head of the house, who happened to see it, and had won him his place.

He walked round the room, looking at each photograph in turn. It seemed incredible that he had no longer any right to an interest in the success of Blackburn's. He could have endured leaving all this when his time at school was up, for that would have been the natural result of the passing of years. But to be transplanted abruptly and with a wrench from his native soil was too much. He went upstairs to pack, suffering from as severe an attack of the blues as any youth of eighteen had experienced since blues were first invented.

51

Jimmy Silver hovered round, while he packed, with expressions of sympathy and bitter remarks concerning Mr Kay and his wicked works, and, when the operation was concluded, helped Kennedy carry his box over to his new house with the air of one seeing a friend off to the parts beyond the equator.

It was ten o'clock by the time the front door of Kay's closed upon its new head. Kennedy went to the matron's sanctum to be instructed in the geography of the house. The matron, a severe lady, whose faith in human nature had been terribly shaken by five years of office in Kay's, showed him his dormitory and study with a lack of geniality which added a deeper tinge of azure to Kennedy's blues. "So you've come to live here, have you?" her manner seemed to say; "well, I pity you, that's all. A nice time you're going to have."

Kennedy spent the half-hour before going to bed in unpacking his box for the second time, and arranging his books and photographs in the study which had been Wayburn's. He had nothing to find fault with in the study. It was as large as the one he had owned at Blackburn's, and, like it, looked out over the school grounds.

At half-past ten the gas gave a flicker and went out, turned off at the main. Kennedy lit a candle and made his way to his dormitory. There now faced him the more than unpleasant task of introducing himself to its inmates. He knew from experience the disconcerting way in which a dormitory greets an intruder. It was difficult to know how to begin matters. It would take a long time, he thought, to explain his presence to their satisfaction.

Fortunately, however, the dormitory was not unprepared. Things get about very quickly in a house. The matron had told the housemaids; the housemaids had handed it on to their ally, the boot boy; the boot boy had told Wren, whom he happened to meet in the passage, and Wren had told everybody else.

There was an uproar going on when Kennedy opened the door, but it died away as he appeared, and the dormitory gazed at the newcomer in absolute and embarrassing silence. Kennedy had not felt so conscious of the public eye being upon him since he had gone out to bat against the M.C.C., on his first appearance in the ranks of the Eckleton eleven. He went to his bed and began to undress without a word, feeling rather than seeing the eyes that were peering at him. When he had completed the performance of disrobing, he blew out the candle and got into bed. The silence was broken by numerous coughs, of that short, suggestive type with which the public schoolboy loves to embarrass his fellow man. From some unidentified corner of the room came a subdued giggle. Then a whispered, "Shut up, you fool!" To which a low voice replied, "All right, I'm not doing anything."

More coughs, and another outbreak of giggling from a fresh quarter.

"Good night," said Kennedy, to the room in general.

There was no reply. The giggler appeared to be rapidly approaching hysterics.

"Shut up that row," said Kennedy.

The giggling ceased.

The atmosphere was charged with suspicion. Kennedy fell asleep fearing that he was going to have trouble with his dormitory before many nights had passed.

53

X

FURTHER EXPERIENCES OF AN EXILE

Breakfast on the following morning was a repetition of the dormitory ordeal. Kennedy walked to his place on Mr Kay's right, feeling that everyone was looking at him, as indeed they were. He understood for the first time the meaning of the expression, "the cynosure of all eyes". He was modest by nature, and felt his position a distinct trial.

He did not quite know what to say or do with regard to his new house-master at this their first meeting in the latter's territory. "Come aboard, sir," occurred to him for a moment as a happy phrase, but he discarded it. To make the situation more awkward, Mr Kay did not observe him at first, being occupied in assailing a riotous fag at the other end of the table, that youth having succeeded, by a dexterous drive in the ribs, in making a friend of his spill half a cup of coffee. Kennedy did not know whether to sit down without a word or to remain standing until Mr Kay had time to attend to him. He would have done better to have sat down; Mr Kay's greeting, when it came, was not worth waiting for.

"Sit down, Kennedy," he said, irritably—rebuking people on an empty stomach always ruffled him. "Sit down, sit down."

Kennedy sat down, and began to toy diffidently with a sausage, remembering, as he did so, certain diatribes of Fenn's against the food at Kay's. As he became more intimate with the sausage, he admitted to himself that Fenn had had reason. Mr Kay meanwhile pounded away in moody silence at a plate of kidneys and bacon. It was one of the many grievances which gave the Kayite material for conversation that Mr Kay had not the courage of his opinions in the matter of food. He insisted that he fed his house luxuriously, but he refused to brave the mysteries of its bill of fare himself.

Fenn had not come down when Kennedy went in to breakfast. He arrived some ten minutes later, when Kennedy had vanquished the sausage, and was keeping body and soul together with bread and marmalade.

54

"I cannot have this, Fenn," snapped Mr Kay; "you must come down in time."

Fenn took the rebuke in silence, cast one glance at the sausage which confronted him, and then pushed it away with such unhesitating rapidity that Mr Kay glared at him as if about to take up the cudgels for the rejected viand. Perhaps he remembered that it scarcely befitted the dignity of a house-master to enter upon a wrangle with a member of his house on the subject of the merits and demerits of sausages, for he refrained, and Fenn was allowed to go on with his meal in peace.

Kennedy's chief anxiety had been with regard to Fenn. True, the latter could hardly blame him for being made head of Kay's, since he had not been consulted in the matter, and, if he had been, would have refused the post with horror; but nevertheless the situation might cause a coolness between them. And if Fenn, the only person in the house with whom he was at all intimate, refused to be on friendly terms, his stay in Kay's would be rendered worse than even he had looked for.

Fenn had not spoken to him at breakfast, but then there was little table talk at Kay's. Perhaps the quality of the food suggested such gloomy reflections that nobody liked to put them into words.

After the meal Fenn ran upstairs to his study. Kennedy followed him, and opened conversation in his direct way with the subject which he had come to discuss.

"I say," he said, "I hope you aren't sick about this. You know I didn't want to bag your place as head of the house."

"My dear chap," said Fenn, "don't apologise. You're welcome to it. Being head of Kay's isn't such a soft job that one is keen on sticking to it."

"All the same—" began Kennedy.

"I knew Kay would get at me somehow, of course. I've been wondering how all the holidays. I didn't think of this. Still, I'm jolly glad it's happened. I now retire into private life, and look on. I've taken years off my life sweating to make this house decent, and now I'm going to take a rest and watch you tearing your hair out over the job. I'm awfully sorry for you. I wish they'd roped in some other victim."

"But you're still a house prefect, I suppose?"

"I believe so, Kay couldn't very well make me a fag again."

"Then you'll help manage things?"

Fenn laughed.

"Will I, by Jove! I'd like to see myself! I don't want to do the heavy martyr business and that sort of thing, but I'm hanged if I'm going to take any more trouble over the house. Haven't you any respect for Mr Kay's feelings? He thinks I can't keep order. Surely you don't want me to go and shatter his pet beliefs? Anyhow, I'm not going to do it. I'm going to play 'villagers and retainers' to your 'hero'. If you do anything wonderful with the house, I shall be standing by ready to cheer. But you don't catch me shoving myself forward. 'Thank Heaven I knows me place,' as the butler in the play says."

Kennedy kicked moodily at the leg of the chair which he was holding. The feeling that his whole world had fallen about his ears was increasing with every hour he spent in Kay's. Last term he and Fenn had been as close friends as you could wish to see. If he had asked Fenn to help him in a tight place then, he knew he could have relied on him. Now his chief desire seemed to be to score off the human race in general, his best friend included. It was a depressing beginning.

"Do you know what the sherry said to the man when he was just going to drink it?" inquired Fenn. "It said, 'Nemo me impune lacessit'. That's how I feel. Kay went out of his way to give me a bad time when I was doing my best to run his house properly, so I don't see that I'm called upon to go out of my way to work for him."

"It's rather rough on me—" Kennedy began. Then a sudden indignation rushed through him. Why should he grovel to Fenn? If Fenn chose to stand out, let him. He was capable of running the house by himself.

"I don't care," he said, savagely. "If you can't see what a cad you're making of yourself, I'm not going to try to show you. You can do what you jolly well please. I'm not dependent on you. I'll make this a decent house off my own bat without your help. If you like looking on, you'd better look on. I'll give you something to look at soon."

He went out, leaving Fenn with mixed feelings. He would have liked to have followed him, taken back what he had said, and formed an offensive alliance against the black sheep of the house—and also, which was just as important, against the slack sheep, who were good for nothing, either at work or play. But his bitterness against the house-master prevented him. He was not going to take his removal from the leadership of Kay's as if nothing had happened.

Meanwhile, in the dayrooms and studies, the house had been holding indignation meetings, and at each it had been unanimously resolved that Kay's had been abominably treated, and that the deposition of Fenn must not be tolerated. Unfortunately, a house cannot do very much when it revolts. It can only show its displeasure in little things, and by an increase of rowdiness. This was the line that Kay's took. Fenn became a popular hero. Fags, until he kicked them for it, showed a tendency to cheer him whenever they saw him. Nothing could paint Mr Kay blacker in the eyes of his house, so that Kennedy came in for all the odium. The same fags who had cheered Fenn hooted him on one occasion as he passed the junior dayroom. Kennedy stopped short, went in, and presented each inmate of the room with six cuts with a swagger-stick. This summary and Captain Kettle-like move had its effect. There was no more hooting. The fags bethought themselves of other ways of showing their disapproval of their new head.

One genius suggested that they might kill two birds with one stone—snub Kennedy and pay a stately compliment to Fenn by applying to the latter for leave to go out of bounds instead of to the former. As the giving of leave "down town" was the prerogative of the head of the house, and of no other, there was a suggestiveness about this mode of procedure which appealed to the junior dayroom.

But the star of the junior dayroom was not in the ascendant. Fenn might have quarrelled with Kennedy, and be extremely indignant at his removal from the headship of the house, but he was not the man to forget to play the game. His policy of non-interference did not include underhand attempts to sap Kennedy's authority. When Gorrick, of the Lower Fourth, the first of the fags to put the ingenious scheme into practice, came to him, still smarting from Kennedy's castigation, Fenn promptly gave him six more cuts, worse than the first, and kicked him out into the passage. Gorrick naturally did not want to spoil a good thing by giving Fenn's game away, so he lay low and said nothing, with the result that Wren and three others met with the same fate, only more so, because Fenn's wrath increased with each visit.

57

Kennedy, of course, heard nothing of this, or he might perhaps have thought better of Fenn. As for the junior dayroom, it was obliged to work off its emotion by jeering Jimmy Silver from the safety of the touchline when the head of Blackburn's was refereeing in a match between the juniors of his house and those of Kay's. Blackburn's happened to win by four goals and eight tries, a result which the patriotic Kay fag attributed solely to favouritism on the part of the referee.

"I like the kids in your house," said Jimmy to Kennedy, after the match, when telling the latter of the incident; "there's no false idea of politeness about them. If they don't like your decisions, they say so in a shrill treble."

"Little beasts," said Kennedy. "I wish I knew who they were. It's hopeless to try and spot them, of course."

XI

THE SENIOR DAYROOM OPENS FIRE

Curiously enough, it was shortly after this that the junior dayroom ceased almost entirely to trouble the head of the house. Not that they turned over new leaves, and modelled their conduct on that of the hero of the Sunday-school story. They were still disorderly, but in a lesser degree; and ragging became a matter of private enterprise among the fags instead of being, as it had threatened to be, an organised revolt against the new head. When a Kay's fag rioted now, he did so with the air of one endeavouring to amuse himself, not as if he were carrying on a holy war against the oppressor.

Kennedy's difficulties were considerably diminished by this change. A head of a house expects the juniors of his house to rag. It is what they are put into the world to do, and there is no difficulty in keeping the thing within decent limits. A revolution is another case altogether. Kennedy was grateful for the change, for it gave him more time to keep an eye on the other members of the house, but he had no idea what had brought it about. As a matter of fact, he had Billy Silver to thank for it. The chief organiser of the movement against Kennedy in the junior dayroom had been the red-haired Wren, who preached war to his fellow fags, partly because he loved to create a disturbance, and partly because Walton, who hated Kennedy, had told him to. Between Wren and Billy Silver a feud had existed since their first meeting. The unsatisfactory conclusion to their encounter in camp had given another lease of life to the feud, and Billy had come back to Kay's with the fixed intention of smiting his auburn-haired foe hip and thigh at the earliest opportunity. Wren's attitude with respect to Kennedy gave him a decent excuse. He had no particular regard for Kennedy. The fact that he was a friend of his brother's was no recommendation. There existed between the two Silvers that feeling which generally exists between an elder and a much younger brother at the same school. Each thought the other a bit of an idiot, and though equal to tolerating him personally, was hanged if he was going to do the same by his friends. In Billy's circle of acquaintances, Jimmy's friends were looked upon with cold suspicion as officious meddlers who would give them lines if they found them out of bounds. The aristocrats with whom Jimmy foregathered barely recognised the existence of Billy's companions. Kennedy's claim to Billy's good offices rested on the fact that they both objected to Wren.

So that, when Wren lifted up his voice in the junior dayroom, and exhorted the fags to go and make a row in the passage outside Kennedy's study, and—from a safe distance, and having previously ensured a means of rapid escape—to fling boots at his door, Billy damped the popular enthusiasm which had been excited by the proposal by kicking Wren with some violence, and begging him not to be an ass. Whereupon they resumed their battle at the point at which it had been interrupted at camp. And when, some five minutes later, Billy, from his seat on his adversary's chest, offered to go through the same performance with anybody else who wished, the junior dayroom came to the conclusion that his feelings with regard to the new head of the house, however foolish and unpatriotic, had better be respected. And the revolution of the fags had fizzled out from that moment.

In the senior dayroom, however, the flag of battle was still unfurled. It was so obvious that Kennedy had been put into the house as a reformer, and the seniors of Kay's had such an objection to being reformed, that trouble was only to be expected. It was the custom in most houses for the head of the house, by right of that position, to be also captain of football. The senior dayroom was aggrieved at Kennedy's taking this post from Fenn. Fenn was in his second year in the school fifteen, and he was the three-quarter who scored most frequently for Eckleton, whereas Kennedy, though practically a certainty for one of the six vacant places in the school scrum, was at present entitled to wear only a second fifteen cap. The claims of Fenn to be captain of Kay's football were strong, Kennedy had begged him to continue in that position more than once. Fenn's persistent refusal had helped to increase the coolness between them, and it had also made things more difficult for Kennedy in the house.

It was on the Monday of the third week of term that Kennedy, at Jimmy Silver's request, arranged a "friendly" between Kay's and Blackburn's. There could be no doubt as to which was the better team (for Blackburn's had been runners up for the Cup the season before), but the better one's opponents the better the practice.

Kennedy wrote out the list and fixed it on the notice board. The match was to be played on the following afternoon.

A football team must generally be made up of the biggest men at the captain's disposal, so it happened that Walton, Perry, Callingham, and the other leaders of dissension in Kay's all figured on the list. The consequence was that the list came in for a good deal of comment in the senior dayroom. There were games every Saturday and Wednesday, and it annoyed Walton and friends that they should have to turn out on an afternoon that was not a half holiday. It was trouble enough playing football on the days when it was compulsory. As for patriotism, no member of the house even pretended to care whether Kay's put a good team into the field or not. The senior dayroom sat talking over the matter till lights-out. When Kennedy came down next morning, he found his list scribbled over with blue pencil, while across it in bold letters ran the single word,

ROT.

He went to his study, wrote out a fresh copy, and pinned it up in place of the old one. He had been early in coming down that morning, and the majority of the Kayites had not seen the defaced notice. The match was fixed for half-past four. At four a thin rain was falling. The weather had been bad for some days, but on this particular afternoon it reached the limit. In addition to being wet, it was also cold, and Kennedy, as he walked over to the grounds, felt that he would be glad when the game was over. He hoped that Blackburn's would be punctual, and congratulated himself on his foresight in securing Mr Blackburn as referee. Some of the staff, when they consented to hold the whistle in a scratch game, invariably kept the teams waiting on the field for half an hour before turning up. Mr Blackburn, an the other hand, was always punctual. He came out of his house just as Kennedy turned in at the school gates.

"Well, Kennedy," he said from the depths of his ulster, the collar of which he had turned up over his ears with a prudence which Kennedy, having come out with only a blazer on over his football clothes, distinctly envied, "I hope your men are not going to be late. I don't think I ever saw a worse day for football. How long were you thinking of playing? Two twenty-fives would be enough for a day like this, I think."

Kennedy consulted with Jimmy Silver, who came up at this moment, and they agreed without argument that twenty-five minutes each way would be the very thing.

"Where are your men?" asked Jimmy. "I've got all our chaps out here, bar Challis, who'll be out in a few minutes. I left him almost changed."

Challis appeared a little later, and joined the rest of Blackburn's team, who were putting in the time and trying to keep warm by running and passing and dropping desultory goals. But, with the exception of Fenn, who stood brooding by himself in the centre of the field, wrapped to the eyes in a huge overcoat, and two other house prefects of Kay's, who strolled up and down looking as if they wished they were in their studies, there was no sign of the missing team.

"I can't make it out," said Kennedy.

"You're sure you put up the right time?" asked Jimmy Silver.

"Yes, quite."

It certainly could not be said that Kay's had had any room for doubt as to the time of the match, for it had appeared in large figures on both notices.

A quarter to five sounded from the college clock.

"We must begin soon," said Mr Blackburn, "or there will not be light enough even for two twenty-fives."

Kennedy felt wretched. Apart from the fact that he was frozen to an icicle and drenched by the rain, he felt responsible for his team, and he could see that Blackburn's men were growing irritated at the delay, though they did their best to conceal it.

"Can't we lend them some subs?" suggested Challis, hopefully.

"All right—if you can raise eleven subs," said Silver. "They've only got four men on the field at present."

Challis subsided.

"Look here," said Kennedy, "I'm going back to the house to see

62

what's up. I'll be back as soon as I can. They must have mistaken the time or something after all."

He rushed back to the house, and flung open the door of the senior dayroom. It was empty.

Kennedy had expected to find his missing men huddled in a semicircle round the fire, waiting for some one to come and tell them that Blackburn's had taken the field, and that they could come out now without any fear of having to wait in the rain for the match to begin. This, he thought, would have been the unselfish policy of Kay's senior dayroom.

But to find nobody was extraordinary.

The thought occurred to him that the team might be changing in their dormitories. He ran upstairs. But all the dormitories were locked, as he might have known they would have been. Coming downstairs again he met his fag, Spencer.

Spencer replied to his inquiry that he had only just come in. He did not know where the team had got to. No, he had not seen any of them.

"Oh, yes, though," he added, as an afterthought, "I met Walton just now. He looked as if he was going down town."

Walton had once licked Spencer, and that vindictive youth thought that this might be a chance of getting back at him.

"Oh," said Kennedy, quietly, "Walton? Did you? Thanks."

Spencer was disappointed at his lack of excitement. His news did not seem to interest him.

Kennedy went back to the football field to inform Jimmy Silver of the result of his investigations.

XII

KENNEDY INTERVIEWS WALTON

"I'm very sorry," he said, when he rejoined the shivering group, "but I'm afraid we shall have to call this match off. There seems to have been a mistake. None of my team are anywhere about. I'm awfully sorry, sir," he added, to Mr Blackburn, "to have given you all this trouble for nothing."

"Not at all, Kennedy. We must try another day."

Mr Blackburn suspected that something untoward had happened in Kay's to cause this sudden defection of the first fifteen of the house. He knew that Kennedy was having a hard time in his new position, and he did not wish to add to his discomfort by calling for an explanation before an audience. It could not be pleasant for Kennedy to feel that his enemies had scored off him. It was best to preserve a discreet silence with regard to the whole affair, and leave him to settle it for himself.

Jimmy Silver was more curious. He took Kennedy off to tea in his study, sat him down in the best chair in front of the fire, and proceeded to urge him to confess everything.

"Now, then, what's it all about?" he asked, briskly, spearing a muffin on the fork and beginning to toast.

"It's no good asking me," said Kennedy. "I suppose it's a put-up job to make me look a fool. I ought to have known something of this kind would happen when I saw what they did to my first notice."

"What was that?"

Kennedy explained.

"This is getting thrilling," said Jimmy. "Just pass that plate. Thanks. What are you going to do about it?"

"I don't know. What would you do?"

"My dear chap, I'd first find out who was at the bottom of it—there's bound to be one man who started the whole thing—and I'd make it my aim in life to give him the warmest ten minutes he'd ever had."

"That sounds all right. But how would you set about it?"

"Why, touch him up, of course. What else would you do? Before the whole house, too."

"Supposing he wouldn't be touched up?"

"Wouldn't be! He'd have to."

"You don't know Kay's, Jimmy. You're thinking what you'd do if this had happened in Blackburn's. The two things aren't the same. Here the man would probably take it like a lamb. The feeling of the house would be against him. He'd find nobody to back him up. That's because Blackburn's is a decent house instead of being a sink like Kay's. If I tried the touching-up before the whole house game with our chaps, the man would probably reply by going for me, assisted by the whole strength of the company."

"Well, dash it all then, all you've got to do is to call a prefects' meeting, and he'll get ten times worse beans from them than he'd have got from you. It's simple."

Kennedy stared into the fire pensively.

"I don't know," he said. "I bar that prefects' meeting business. It always seems rather feeble to me, lugging in a lot of chaps to help settle some one you can't manage yourself. I want to carry this job through on my own."

"Then you'd better scrap with the man."

"I think I will."

Silver stared.

"Don't be an ass," he said. "I was only rotting. You can't go fighting all over the shop as if you were a fag. You'd lose your prefect's cap if it came out."

"I could wear my topper," said Kennedy, with a grin. "You see," he added, "I've not much choice. I must do something. If I took no notice of this business there'd be no holding the house. I should be ragged to death. It's no good talking about it. Personally, I should prefer touching the chap up to fighting him, and I shall try it on. But he's not likely to meet me half-way. And if he doesn't there'll be an interesting turn-up, and you shall hold the watch. I'll send a kid round to fetch you when things look like starting. I must go now to interview my missing men. So long. Mind you slip round directly I send for you."

"Wait a second. Don't be in such a beastly hurry. Who's the chap you're going to fight?"

"I don't know yet. Walton, I should think. But I don't know."

"Walton! By Jove, it'll be worth seeing, anyhow, if we are both sacked for it when the Old Man finds out."

Kennedy returned to his study and changed his football boots for a pair of gymnasium shoes. For the job he had in hand it was necessary that he should move quickly, and football boots are a nuisance on a board floor. When he had changed, he called Spencer.

"Go down to the senior dayroom," he said, "and tell MacPherson I want to see him."

MacPherson was a long, weak-looking youth. He had been put down to play for the house that day, and had not appeared.

"MacPherson!" said the fag, in a tone of astonishment, "not Walton?"

He had been looking forward to the meeting between Kennedy and his ancient foe, and to have a miserable being like MacPherson offered as a substitute disgusted him.

"If you have no objection," said Kennedy, politely, "I may want you to fetch Walton later on."

Spencer vanished, hopeful once more.

"Come in, MacPherson," said Kennedy, on the arrival of the long one; "shut the door."

MacPherson did so, feeling as if he were paying a visit to the dentist. As long as there had been others with him in this affair he had looked on it as a splendid idea. But to be singled out like this was quite a different thing.

"Now," said Kennedy, "Why weren't you on the field this afternoon?"

"I—er—I was kept in."

"How long?"

"Oh—er—till about five."

"What do you call about five?"

"About twenty-five to," he replied, despondently.

"Now look here," said Kennedy, briskly, "I'm just going to explain to you exactly how I stand in this business, so you'd better attend. I didn't ask to be made head of this sewage depot. If I could have had any choice, I wouldn't have touched a Kayite with a barge-pole. But since I am head, I'm going to be it, and the sooner you and your senior dayroom crew realise it the better. This sort of thing isn't going on. I want to know now who it was put up this job. You wouldn't have the cheek to start a thing like this yourself. Who was it?"

"Well—er—"

"You'd better say, and be quick, too. I can't wait. Whoever it was. I shan't tell him you told me. And I shan't tell Kay. So now you can go ahead. Who was it?"

"Well—er—Walton."

"I thought so. Now you can get out. If you see Spencer, send him here."

Spencer, curiously enough, was just outside the door. So close to it, indeed, that he almost tumbled in when MacPherson opened it.

"Go and fetch Walton," said Kennedy.

Spencer dashed off delightedly, and in a couple of minutes Walton appeared. He walked in with an air of subdued defiance, and slammed the door.

"Don't bang the door like that," said Kennedy. "Why didn't you turn out today?"

"I was kept in."

"Couldn't you get out in time to play?"

"No."

"When did you get out?"

"Six."

"Not before?"

"I said six."

"Then how did you manage to go down town—without leave, by the way, but that's a detail—at half-past five?"

"All right," said Walton; "better call me a liar."

"Good suggestion," said Kennedy, cheerfully; "I will."

"It's all very well," said Walton. "You know jolly well you can say anything you like. I can't do anything to you. You'd have me up before the prefects."

"Not a bit of it. This is a private affair between ourselves. I'm not going to drag the prefects into it. You seem to want to make this house worse than it is. I want to make it more or less decent. We can't both have what we want."

There was a pause.

"When would it be convenient for you to be touched up before the whole house?" inquired Kennedy, pleasantly.

"What?"

"Well, you see, it seems the only thing. I must take it out of some one for this house-match business, and you started it. Will tonight suit you, after supper?"

"You'll get it hot if you try to touch me."

"We'll see."

68

"You'd funk taking me on in a scrap," said Walton.

"Would I? As a matter of fact, a scrap would suit me just as well. Better. Are you ready now?"

"Quite, thanks," sneered Walton. "I've knocked you out before, and I'll do it again."

"Oh, then it was you that night at camp? I thought so. I spotted your style. Hitting a chap when he wasn't ready, you know, and so on. Now, if you'll wait a minute, I'll send across to Blackburn's for Silver. I told him I should probably want him as a time-keeper tonight."

"What do you want with Silver. Why won't Perry do?"

"Thanks, I'm afraid Perry's time-keeping wouldn't be impartial enough. Silver, I think, if you don't mind."

Spencer was summoned once more, and despatched to Blackburn's. He returned with Jimmy.

"Come in, Jimmy," said Kennedy. "Run away, Spencer. Walton and I are just going to settle a point of order which has arisen, Jimmy. Will you hold the watch? We ought just to have time before tea."

"Where?" asked Silver.

"My dormitory would be the best place. We can move the beds. I'll go and get the keys."

Kennedy's dormitory was the largest in the house. After the beds had been moved back, there was a space in the middle of fifteen feet one way, and twelve the other—not a large ring, but large enough for two fighters who meant business.

Walton took off his coat, waistcoat, and shirt. Kennedy, who was still in football clothes, removed his blazer.

"Half a second," said Jimmy Silver—"what length rounds?"

"Two minutes?" said Kennedy to Walton.

"All right," growled Walton.

"Two minutes, then, and half a minute in between."

69

"Are you both ready?" asked Jimmy, from his seat on the chest of drawers.

Kennedy and Walton advanced into the middle of the impromptu ring.

There was dead silence for a moment.

"Time!" said Jimmy Silver.

70

XIII

THE FIGHT IN THE DORMITORY

Stating it broadly, fighters may be said to be divided into two classes—those who are content to take two blows if they can give three in return, and those who prefer to receive as little punishment as possible, even at the expense of scoring fewer points themselves. Kennedy's position, when Jimmy Silver called time, was peculiar. On all the other occasions on which he had fought—with the gloves on in the annual competition, and at the assault-at-arms—he had gone in for the policy of taking all that the other man liked to give him, and giving rather more in exchange. Now, however, he was obliged to alter his whole style. For a variety of reasons it was necessary that he should come out of this fight with as few marks as possible. To begin with, he represented, in a sense, the Majesty of the Law. He was tackling Walton more by way of an object-lesson to the Kayite mutineers than for his own personal satisfaction. The object-lesson would lose in impressiveness if he were compelled to go about for a week or so with a pair of black eyes, or other adornments of a similar kind. Again—and this was even more important—if he was badly marked the affair must come to the knowledge of the headmaster. Being a prefect, and in the sixth form, he came into contact with the Head every day, and the disclosure of the fact that he had been engaged in a pitched battle with a member of his house, who was, in addition to other disadvantages, very low down in the school, would be likely to lead to unpleasantness. A school prefect of Eckleton was supposed to be hedged about with so much dignity that he could quell turbulent inferiors with a glance. The idea of one of the august body lowering himself to the extent of emphasising his authority with the bare knuckle would scandalise the powers.

So Kennedy, rising at the call of time from the bed on which he sat, came up to the scratch warily.

Walton, on the other hand, having everything to gain and nothing to lose, and happy in the knowledge that no amount of bruises could do him any harm, except physically, came on with the evident intention of making a hurricane fight of it. He had very little science as a boxer. Heavy two-handed slogging was his forte, and, as the majority of his opponents up to the present had not had sufficient skill to discount his strength, he had found this a very successful line of action. Kennedy and he had never had the gloves on together. In the competition of the previous year both had entered in their respective classes, Kennedy as a lightweight, Walton in the middles, and both, after reaching the semi-final, had been defeated by the narrowest of margins by men who had since left the school. That had been in the previous Easter term, and, while Walton had remained much the same as regards weight and strength, Kennedy, owing to a term of hard bowling and a summer holiday spent in the open, had filled out. They were now practically on an equality, as far as weight was concerned. As for condition, that was all in favour of Kennedy. He played football in his spare time. Walton, on the days when football was not compulsory, smoked cigarettes.

Neither of the pair showed any desire to open the fight by shaking hands. This was not a friendly spar. It was business. The first move was made by Walton, who feinted with his right and dashed in to fight at close quarters. It was not a convincing feint. At any rate, it did not deceive Kennedy. He countered with his left, and swung his right at the body with all the force he could put into the hit. Walton went back a pace, sparred for a moment, then came in again, hitting heavily. Kennedy's counter missed its mark this time. He just stopped a round sweep of Walton's right, ducked to avoid a similar effort of his left, and they came together in a clinch.

In a properly regulated glove-fight, the referee, on observing the principals clinch, says, "Break away there, break away," in a sad, reproachful voice, and the fighters separate without demur, being very much alive to the fact that, as far as that contest is concerned, their destinies are in his hands, and that any bad behaviour in the ring will lose them the victory. But in an impromptu turn-up like this one, the combatants show a tendency to ignore the rules so carefully mapped out by the present Marquess of Queensberry's grandfather, and revert to the conditions of warfare under which Cribb and Spring won their battles. Kennedy and Walton, having clinched, proceeded to wrestle up and down the room, while Jimmy Silver looked on from his eminence in pained surprise at the sight of two men, who knew the rules of the ring, so far forgetting themselves.

To do Kennedy justice, it was not his fault. He was only acting in self-defence. Walton had started the hugging. Also, he had got the under-grip, which, when neither man knows a great deal of the science of wrestling, generally means victory. Kennedy was quite sure that he could not throw his antagonist, but he hung on in the knowledge that the round must be over shortly, when Walton would have to loose him.

"Time," said Jimmy Silver.

Kennedy instantly relaxed his grip, and in that instant Walton swung him off his feet, and they came down together with a crash that shook the room. Kennedy was underneath, and, as he fell, his head came into violent contact with the iron support of a bed.

Jimmy Silver sprang down from his seat.

"What are you playing at, Walton? Didn't you hear me call time? It was a beastly foul—the worst I ever saw. You ought to be sacked for a thing like that. Look here, Kennedy, you needn't go on. I disqualify Walton for fouling."

The usually genial James stammered with righteous indignation.

Kennedy sat down on a bed, dizzily.

"No," he said; "I'm going on."

"But he fouled you."

"I don't care. I'll look after myself. Is it time yet?"

"Ten seconds more, if you really are going on."

He climbed back on to the chest of drawers.

"Time."

Kennedy came up feeling weak and sick. The force with which he had hit his head on the iron had left him dazed.

Walton rushed in as before. He had no chivalrous desire to spare his man by way of compensation for fouling him. What monopolised his attention was the evident fact that Kennedy was in a bad way, and that a little strenuous infighting might end the affair in the desired manner.

It was at this point that Kennedy had reason to congratulate himself on donning gymnasium shoes. They gave him that extra touch of lightness which enabled him to dodge blows which he was too weak to parry. Everything was vague and unreal to him. He seemed to be looking on at a fight between Walton and some stranger.

Then the effect of his fall began to wear off. He could feel himself growing stronger. Little by little his head cleared, and he began once more to take a personal interest in the battle. It is astonishing what a power a boxer, who has learnt the art carefully, has of automatic fighting. The expert gentleman who fights under the pseudonym of "Kid M'Coy" once informed the present writer that in one of his fights he was knocked down by such a severe hit that he remembered nothing further, and it was only on reading the paper next morning that he found, to his surprise, that he had fought four more rounds after the blow, and won the battle handsomely on points. Much the same thing happened to Kennedy. For the greater part of the second round he fought without knowing it. When Jimmy Silver called time he was in as good case as ever, and the only effects of the blow on his head were a vast lump underneath the hair, and a settled determination to win or perish. In a few minutes the bell would ring for tea, and all his efforts would end in nothing. It was no good fighting a draw with Walton if he meant to impress the house. He knew exactly what Rumour, assisted by Walton, would make of the affair in that case. "Have you heard the latest?" A would ask of B. "Why, Kennedy tried to touch Walton up for not playing footer, and Walton went for him and would have given him frightful beans, only they had to go down to tea." There must be none of that sort of thing.

"Time," said Jimmy Silver, breaking in on his meditations.

It was probably the suddenness and unexpectedness of it that took Walton aback. Up till now his antagonist had been fighting strictly on the defensive, and was obviously desirous of escaping punishment as far as might be possible. And then the fall at the end of round one had shaken him up, so that he could hardly fight at all at their second meeting. Walton naturally expected that it would be left to him to do the leading in round three. Instead of this, however, Kennedy opened the round with such a lightning attack that Walton was all abroad in a moment. In his most scientific mood he had never had the remotest notion of how to guard. He was aggressive and nothing else. Attacked by a quick hitter, he was

74

useless. Three times Kennedy got through his guard with his left. The third hit staggered him. Before he could recover, Kennedy had got his right in, and down went Walton in a heap.

He was up again as soon as he touched the boards, and down again almost as soon as he was up. Kennedy was always a straight hitter, and now a combination of good cause and bad temper—for the thought of the foul in the first round had stirred what was normally a more or less placid nature into extreme viciousness—lent a vigour to his left arm to which he had hitherto been a stranger. He did not use his right again. It was not needed.

Twice more Walton went down. He was still down when Jimmy Silver called time. When the half-minute interval between the rounds was over, he stated that he was not going on.

Kennedy looked across at him as he sat on a bed dabbing tenderly at his face with a handkerchief, and was satisfied with the success of his object-lesson. From his own face the most observant of headmasters could have detected no evidence that he had been engaged in a vulgar fight. Walton, on the other hand, looked as if he had been engaged in several—all violent. Kennedy went off to his study to change, feeling that he had advanced a long step on the thorny path that led to the Perfect House.

XIV

FENN RECEIVES A LETTER

But the step was not such a very long one after all. What it amounted to was simply this, that open rebellion ceased in Kay's. When Kennedy put up the list on the notice-board for the third time, which he did on the morning following his encounter with Walton, and wrote on it that the match with Blackburn's would take place that afternoon, his team turned out like lambs, and were duly defeated by thirty-one points. He had to play a substitute for Walton, who was rather too battered to be of any real use in the scrum; but, with that exception, the team that entered the field was the same that should have entered it the day before.

But his labours in the Augean stables of Kay's were by no means over. Practically they had only begun. The state of the house now was exactly what it had been under Fenn. When Kennedy had taken over the reins, Kay's had become on the instant twice as bad as it had been before. By his summary treatment of the revolution, he had, so to speak, wiped off this deficit. What he had to do now was to begin to improve things. Kay's was now in its normal state—slack, rowdy in an underhand way, and utterly useless to the school. It was "up to" Kennedy, as they say in America, to start in and make something presentable and useful out of these unpromising materials.

What annoyed him more than anything else was the knowledge that if only Fenn chose to do the square thing and help him in his work, the combination would be irresistible. It was impossible to make any leeway to speak of by himself. If Fenn would only forget his grievances and join forces with him, they could electrify the house.

Fenn, however, showed no inclination to do anything of the kind. He and Kennedy never spoke to one another now except when it was absolutely unavoidable, and then they behaved with that painful politeness in which the public schoolman always wraps himself as in a garment when dealing with a friend with whom he has quarrelled.

On the Walton episode Fenn had made no comment, though it is probable that he thought a good deal.

It was while matters were in this strained condition that Fenn received a letter from his elder brother. This brother had been at Eckleton in his time—School House—and had left five years before to go to Cambridge. Cambridge had not taught him a great deal, possibly because he did not meet the well-meant efforts of his tutor half-way. The net result of his three years at King's was—imprimis, a cricket blue, including a rather lucky eighty-three at Lord's; secondly, a very poor degree; thirdly and lastly, a taste for literature and the drama—he had been a prominent member of the Footlights Club. When he came down he looked about him for some occupation which should combine in happy proportions a small amount of work and a large amount of salary, and, finding none, drifted into journalism, at which calling he had been doing very fairly ever since.

"Dear Bob," the letter began. Fenn's names were Robert Mowbray, the second of which he had spent much of his time in concealing. "Just a line."

The elder Fenn always began his letters with these words, whether they ran to one sheet or eight. In the present case the screed was not particularly long.

"Do you remember my reading you a bit of an opera I was writing? Well, I finished it, and, after going the round of most of the managers, who chucked it with wonderful unanimity, it found an admirer in Higgs, the man who took the part of the duke in The Outsider. Luckily, he happened to be thinking of starting on his own in opera instead of farce, and there's a part in mine which fits him like a glove. So he's going to bring it out at the Imperial in the spring, and by way of testing the piece—trying it on the dog, as it were—he means to tour with it. Now, here's the point of this letter. We start at Eckleton next Wednesday. We shall only be there one night, for we go on to Southampton on Thursday. I suppose you couldn't come and see it? I remember Peter Brown, who got the last place in the team the year I got my cricket colours, cutting out of his house (Kay's, by the way) and going down town to see a piece at the theatre. I'm bound to admit he got sacked for it, but still, it shows that it can be done. All the same, I shouldn't try it on if I were you. You'll be able to read all about the 'striking success' and

77

'unrestrained enthusiasm' in the Eckleton Mirror on Thursday. Mind you buy a copy."

The rest of the letter was on other subjects. It took Fenn less than a minute to decide to patronise that opening performance. He was never in the habit of paying very much attention to risks when he wished to do anything, and now he felt as if he cared even less than usual what might be the outcome of the adventure. Since he had ceased to be on speaking terms with Kennedy, he had found life decidedly dull. Kennedy had been his only intimate friend. He had plenty of acquaintances, as a first eleven and first fifteen man usually has, but none of them were very entertaining. Consequently he welcomed the idea of a break in the monotony of affairs. The only thing that had broken it up to the present had been a burglary at the school house. Some enterprising marauder had broken in a week before and gone off with a few articles of value from the headmaster's drawing-room. But the members of the school house had talked about this episode to such an extent that the rest of the school had dropped off the subject, exhausted, and declined to discuss it further. And things had become monotonous once more.

Having decided to go, Fenn began to consider how he should do it. And here circumstances favoured him. It happened that on the evening on which his brother's play was to be produced the headmaster was giving his once-a-term dinner to the house-prefects. This simplified matters wonderfully. The only time when his absence from the house was at all likely to be discovered would be at prayers, which took place at half-past nine. The prefects' dinner solved this difficulty for him. Kay would not expect him to be at prayers, thinking he was over at the Head's, while the Head, if he noticed his absence at all, would imagine that he was staying away from the dinner owing to a headache or some other malady. It seemed tempting Providence not to take advantage of such an excellent piece of luck. For the rest, detection was practically impossible. Kennedy's advent to the house had ousted Fenn from the dormitory in which he had slept hitherto, and, there being no bed available in any of the other dormitories, he had been put into the spare room usually reserved for invalids whose invalidism was not of a sufficiently infectious kind to demand their removal to the infirmary. As for getting back into the house, he would leave the window of his study unfastened. He could easily climb on to the window-ledge, and so to bed without let or hindrance.

The distance from Kay's to the town was a mile and a half. If he started at the hour when he should have been starting for the school house, he would arrive just in time to see the curtain go up.

Having settled these facts definitely in his mind, he got his books together and went over to school.

79

XV

DOWN TOWN

Fenn arrived at the theatre a quarter of an hour before the curtain rose. Going down a gloomy alley of the High Street, he found himself at the stage door, where he made inquiries of a depressed-looking man with a bad cold in the head as to the whereabouts of his brother. It seemed that he was with Mr Higgs. If he would wait, said the door-keeper, his name should be sent up. Fenn waited, while the door-keeper made polite conversation by describing his symptoms to him in a hoarse growl. Presently the minion who had been despatched to the upper regions with Fenn's message returned. Would he go upstairs, third door on the left. Fenn followed the instructions, and found himself in a small room, a third of which was filled by a huge iron-bound chest, another third by a very stout man and a dressing-table, while the rest of the space was comparatively empty, being occupied by a wooden chair with three legs. On this seat his brother was trying to balance himself, giving what part of his attention was not required for this feat to listening to some story the fat man was telling him. Fenn had heard his deep voice booming as he went up the passage.

His brother did the honours.

"Glad to see you, glad to see you," said Mr Higgs, for the fat man was none other than that celebrity. "Take a seat."

Fenn sat down on the chest and promptly tore his trousers on a jagged piece of iron.

"These provincial dressing-rooms!" said Mr Higgs, by way of comment. "No room! Never any room! No chairs! Nothing!"

He spoke in short, quick sentences, and gasped between each. Fenn said it really didn't matter—he was quite comfortable.

"Haven't they done anything about it?" asked Fenn's brother, resuming the conversation which Fenn's entrance had interrupted. "We've been having a burglary here," he explained. "Somebody got into the theatre last night through a window. I don't know what they expected to find."

"Why," said Fenn, "we've had a burglar up our way too. Chap broke into the school house and went through the old man's drawing-room. The school house men have been talking about nothing else ever since. I wonder if it's the same crew."

Mr Higgs turned in his chair, and waved a stick of grease paint impressively to emphasise his point.

"There," he said. "There! What I've been saying all along. No doubt of it. Organised gang. And what are the police doing? Nothing, sir, nothing. Making inquiries. Rot! What's the good of inquiries?"

Fenn's brother suggested mildly that inquiries were a good beginning. You must start somehow. Mr Higgs scouted the idea.

"There ought not to be any doubt, sir. They ought to know. To KNOW," he added, with firmness.

At this point there filtered through the closed doors the strains of the opening chorus.

"By Jove, it's begun!" said Fenn's brother. "Come on, Bob."

"Where are we going to?" asked Fenn, as he followed. "The wings?"

But it seemed that the rules of Mr Higgs' company prevented any outsider taking up his position in that desirable quarter. The only place from which it was possible to watch the performance, except by going to the front of the house, was the "flies," situated near the roof of the building.

Fenn found all the pleasures of novelty in watching the players from this lofty position. Judged by the cold light of reason, it was not the best place from which to see a play. It was possible to gain only a very foreshortened view of the actors. But it was a change after sitting "in front".

The piece was progressing merrily. The gifted author, at first silent and pale, began now to show signs of gratification. Now and again he chuckled as some jeu de mots hit the mark and drew a quick gust of laughter from the unseen audience. Occasionally he would nudge Fenn to draw his attention to some good bit of dialogue which was approaching. He was obviously enjoying himself.

81

The advent of Mr Higgs completed his satisfaction, for the audience greeted the comedian with roars of applause. As a rule Eckleton took its drama through the medium of third-rate touring companies, which came down with plays that had not managed to attract London to any great extent, and were trying to make up for failures in the metropolis by long tours in the provinces. It was seldom that an actor of the Higgs type paid the town a visit, and in a play, too, which had positively never appeared before on any stage. Eckleton appreciated the compliment.

"Listen," said Fenn's brother. "Isn't that just the part for him? It's just like he was in the dressing-room, eh? Short sentences and everything. The funny part of it is that I didn't know the man when I wrote the play. It was all luck."

Mr Higgs' performance sealed the success of the piece. The house laughed at everything he said. He sang a song in his gasping way, and they laughed still more. Fenn's brother became incoherent with delight. The verdict of Eckleton was hardly likely to affect London theatre-goers, but it was very pleasant notwithstanding. Like every playwright with his first piece, he had been haunted by the idea that his dialogue "would not act", that, however humorous it might be to a reader, it would fall flat when spoken. There was no doubt now as to whether the lines sounded well.

At the beginning of the second act the great Higgs was not on the stage, Fenn's brother knowing enough of the game not to bring on his big man too soon. He had not to enter for ten minutes or so. The author, who had gone down to see him during the interval, stayed in the dressing-room. Fenn, however, who wanted to see all of the piece that he could, went up to the "flies" again.

It occurred to him when he got there that he would see more if he took the seat which his brother had been occupying. It would give him much the same view of the stage, and a wider view of the audience. He thought it would be amusing to see how the audience looked from the "flies".

Mr W. S. Gilbert once wrote a poem about a certain bishop who, while fond of amusing himself, objected to his clergy doing likewise. And the consequence was that whenever he did so amuse himself, he was always haunted by a phantom curate, who joined him in his pleasures, much to his dismay. On one occasion he stopped to watch a Punch and Judy show,

And heard, as Punch was being treated penally,
That phantom curate laughing all hyaenally.

The disgust and panic of this eminent cleric was as nothing compared with that of Fenn, when, shifting to his brother's seat, he got the first clear view he had had of the audience. In a box to the left of the dress-circle sat, "laughing all hyaenally", the following distinguished visitors:

> *Mr Mulholland of No. 7 College Buildings.*
> *Mr Raynes of No. 4 ditto,*
> *and*
> *Mr Kay.*

Fenn drew back like a flash, knocking his chair over as he did so.

"Giddy, sir?" said a stage hand, pleasantly. "Bless you, lots of gents is like that when they comes up here. Can't stand the 'eight, they can't. You'll be all right in a jiffy."

"Yes. It—it is rather high, isn't it?" said Fenn. "Awful glare, too."

He picked up his chair and sat down well out of sight of the box. Had they seen him? he wondered. Then common sense returned to him. They could not possibly have seen him. Apart from any other reasons, he had only been in his brother's seat for half-a-dozen seconds. No. He was all right so far. But he would have to get back to the house, and at once. With three of the staff, including his own house-master, ranging the town, things were a trifle too warm for comfort. He wondered it had not occurred to him that, with a big attraction at the theatre, some of the staff might feel an inclination to visit it.

He did not stop to say goodbye to his brother. Descending from his perch, he hurried to the stage door.

"It's in the toobs that I feel it, sir." said the door-keeper, as he let him out, resuming their conversation as if they had only just parted. Fenn hurried off without waiting to hear more.

It was drizzling outside, and there was a fog. Not a "London particular", but quite thick enough to make it difficult to see where one was going. People and vehicles passed him, vague phantoms in the darkness. Occasionally the former collided with him. He began to wish he had not accepted his brother's invitation. The unexpected sight of the three masters had shaken his nerve. Till then only the romantic, adventurous side of the expedition had struck him. Now the risks began to loom larger in his mind. It was all very well, he felt, to think, as he had done, that he would be expelled if found out, but that all the same he would risk it. Detection then had seemed a remote contingency. With three masters in the offing it became at least a possibility. The melancholy case of Peter Brown seemed to him now to have a more personal significance for him.

Wrapped in these reflections, he lost his way.

He did not realise this for some time. It was borne in upon him when the road he was taking suddenly came to an abrupt end in a blank wall. Instead of being, as he had fancied, in the High Street, he must have branched off into some miserable blind alley.

More than ever he wished he had not come. Eckleton was not a town that took up a great deal of room on the map of England, but it made up for small dimensions by the eccentricity with which it had been laid out. On a dark and foggy night, to one who knew little of its geography, it was a perfect maze.

Fenn had wandered some way when the sound of someone whistling a popular music-hall song came to him through the gloom. He had never heard anything more agreeable.

"I say," he shouted at a venture, "can you tell me the way to the High Street?"

The whistler stopped in the middle of a bar, and presently Fenn saw a figure sidling towards him in what struck him as a particularly furtive manner.

"Wot's thet, gav'nor?"

"Can you tell me where the High Street is? I've lost my way."

The vague figure came closer.

"'Igh Street? Yus; yer go—"

A hand shot out, Fenn felt a sharp wrench in the region of his waistcoat, and a moment later the stranger had vanished into the fog with the prefect's watch and chain.

Fenn forgot his desire to return to the High Street. He forgot everything except that he wished to catch the fugitive, maltreat him, and retrieve his property. He tore in the direction whence came the patter of retreating foot-steps.

There were moments when he thought he had him, when he could hear the sound of his breathing. But the fog was against him. Just as he was almost on his man's heels, the fugitive turned sharply into a street which was moderately well lighted. Fenn turned after him. He had just time to recognise the street as his goal, the High Street, when somebody, walking unexpectedly out of the corner house, stood directly in his path. Fenn could not stop himself. He charged the man squarely, clutched him to save himself, and they fell in a heap on the pavement.

XVI

WHAT HAPPENED TO FENN

Fenn was up first. Many years' experience of being tackled at full speed on the football field had taught him how to fall. The stranger, whose football days, if he had ever had any, were long past, had gone down with a crash, and remained on the pavement, motionless. Fenn was conscious of an ignoble impulse to fly without stopping to chat about the matter. Then he was seized with a gruesome fear that he had injured the man seriously, which vanished when the stranger sat up. His first words were hardly of the sort that one would listen to from choice. His first printable expression, which did not escape him until he had been speaking some time, was in the nature of an official bulletin.

"You've broken my neck," said he.

Fenn renewed his apologies and explanations.

"Your watch!" cried the man in a high, cracked voice. "Don't stand there talking about your watch, but help me up. What do I care about your watch? Why don't you look where you are going to? Now then, now then, don't hoist me as if I were a hod of bricks. That's right. Now help me indoors, and go away."

Fenn supported him while he walked lamely into the house. He was relieved to find that there was nothing more the matter with him than a shaking and a few bruises.

"Door on the left," said the injured one.

Fenn led him down the passage and into a small sitting-room. The gas was lit, and as he turned it up he saw that the stranger was a man well advanced in years. He had grey hair that was almost white. His face was not a pleasant one. It was a mass of lines and wrinkles from which a physiognomist would have deduced uncomplimentary conclusions as to his character. Fenn had little skill in that way, but he felt that for some reason he disliked the man, whose eyes, which were small and extraordinarily bright, gave rather an eerie look to his face.

"Go away, go away," he kept repeating savagely from his post on the shabby sofa on which Fenn had deposited him.

"But are you all right? Can't I get you something?" asked the Eckletonian.

"Go away, go away," repeated the man.

Conversation on these lines could never be really attractive. Fenn turned to go. As he closed the door and began to feel his way along the dark passage, he heard the key turn in the lock behind him. The man could not, he felt, have been very badly hurt if he were able to get across the room so quickly. The thought relieved him somewhat. Nobody likes to have the maiming even of the most complete stranger on his mind. The sensation of relief lasted possibly three seconds. Then it flashed upon him that in the excitement of the late interview he had forgotten his cap. That damaging piece of evidence lay on the table in the sitting-room, and between him and it was a locked door.

He groped his way back, and knocked. No sound came from the room.

"I say," he cried, "you might let me have my cap. I left it on the table."

No reply.

Fenn half thought of making a violent assault on the door. He refrained on reflecting that it would be useless. If he could break it open—which, in all probability, he could not—there would be trouble such as he had never come across in his life. He was not sure it would not be an offence for which he would be rendered liable to fine or imprisonment. At any rate, it would mean the certain detection of his visit to the town. So he gave the thing up, resolving to return on the morrow and reopen negotiations. For the present, what he had to do was to get safely back to his house. He had lost his watch, his cap with his name in it was in the hands of an evil old man who evidently bore him a grudge, and he had to run the gauntlet of three house-masters and get to bed via a study-window. Few people, even after the dullest of plays, have returned from the theatre so disgusted with everything as did Fenn. Reviewing the situation as he ran with long, easy strides over the road that led to Kay's, he found it devoid of any kind of comfort. Unless his mission in quest of the cap should prove successful, he was in a tight place.

87

It is just as well that the gift of second sight is accorded to but few. If Fenn could have known at this point that his adventures were only beginning, that what had taken place already was but as the overture to a drama, it is possible that he would have thrown up the sponge for good and all, entered Kay's by way of the front door—after knocking up the entire household—and remarked, in answer to his house-master's excited questions, "Enough! Enough! I am a victim of Fate, a Toad beneath the Harrow. Sack me tomorrow, if you like, but for goodness' sake let me get quietly to bed now."

As it was, not being able to "peep with security into futurity," he imagined that the worst was over.

He began to revise this opinion immediately on turning in at Kay's gate. He had hardly got half-way down the drive when the front door opened and two indistinct figures came down the steps. As they did so his foot slipped off the grass border on which he was running to deaden the noise of his steps, and grated sharply on the gravel.

"What's that?" said a voice. The speaker was Mr Kay.

"What's what?" replied a second voice which he recognised as Mr Mulholland's.

"Didn't you hear a noise?"

"'I heard the water lapping on the crag,'" replied Mr Mulholland, poetically.

"It was over there," persisted Mr Kay. "I am certain I heard something—positively certain, Mulholland. And after that burglary at the school house—"

He began to move towards the spot where Fenn lay crouching behind a bush. Mr Mulholland followed, mildly amused. They were a dozen yards away when Fenn, debating in his mind whether it would not be better—as it would certainly be more dignified—for him to rise and deliver himself up to justice instead of waiting to be discovered wallowing in the damp grass behind a laurel bush, was aware of something soft and furry pressing against his knuckles. A soft purring sound reached his ears.

He knew at once who it was—Thomas Edward, the matron's cat, ever a staunch friend of his. Many a time had they taken tea together in his study in happier days. The friendly animal had sought him out in his hiding-place, and was evidently trying to intimate that the best thing they could do now would be to make a regular night of it.

Fenn, as I have said, liked and respected Thomas. In ordinary circumstances he would not have spoken an unfriendly word to him. But things were desperate now, and needed remedies to match.

Very softly he passed his hand down the delighted animal's back until he reached his tail. Then, stifling with an effort all the finer feelings which should have made such an act impossible, he administered so vigorous a tweak to that appendage that Thomas, with one frenzied yowl, sprang through the bush past the two masters and vanished at full speed into the opposite hedge.

"My goodness!" said Mr Kay, starting back.

It was a further shock to Fenn to find how close he was to the laurel.

> "'Goodness me,
>   Why, what was that?
> Silent be,
>   It was the cat,'"

chanted Mr Mulholland, who was in poetical vein after the theatre.

"It was a cat!" gasped Mr Kay.

"So I am disposed to imagine. What lungs! We shall be having the R.S.P.C.A. down on us if we aren't careful. They must have heard that noise at the headquarters of the Society, wherever they are. Well, if your zeal for big game hunting is satisfied, and you don't propose to follow the vocalist through that hedge, I think I will be off. Good night. Good piece, wasn't it?"

"Excellent. Good night, Mulholland."

"By the way, I wonder if the man who wrote it is a relation of our Fenn. It may be his brother—I believe he writes. You probably remember him when he was here. He was before my time. Talking of Fenn, how do you find the new arrangement answer? Is Kennedy an improvement?"

"Kennedy," said Mr Kay, "is a well-meaning boy, I think. Quite well-meaning. But he lacks ability, in my opinion. I have had to speak to him on several occasions on account of disturbances amongst the juniors. Once I found two boys actually fighting in the junior dayroom. I was very much annoyed about it."

"And where was Kennedy while this was going on? Was he holding the watch?"

"The watch?" said Mr Kay, in a puzzled tone of voice. "Kennedy was over at the gymnasium when it occurred."

"Then it was hardly his fault that the fight took place."

"My dear Mulholland, if the head of a house is efficient, fights should be impossible. Even when he is not present, his influence, his prestige, so to speak, should be sufficient to restrain the boys under him."

Mr Mulholland whistled softly.

"So that's your idea of what the head of your house should be like, is it? Well, I know of one fellow who would have been just your man. Unfortunately, he is never likely to come to school at Eckleton."

"Indeed?" said Mr Kay, with interest. "Who is that? Where did you meet him? What school is he at?"

"I never said I had met him. I only go by what I have heard of him. And as far as I know, he is not at any school. He was a gentleman of the name of Napoleon Bonaparte. He might just have been equal to the arduous duties which devolve upon the head of your house. Goodnight."

And Fenn heard his footsteps crunch the gravel as he walked away. A minute later the front door shut, and there was a rattle. Mr Kay had put the chain up and retired for the night.

Fenn lay where he was for a short while longer. Then he rose, feeling very stiff and wet, and crept into one of the summer-houses which stood in Mr Kay's garden. Here he sat for an hour and a half, at the end of which time, thinking that Mr Kay must be asleep, he started out to climb into the house.

His study was on the first floor. A high garden-seat stood directly beneath the window and acted as a convenient ladder. It was easy to get from this on to the window-ledge. Once there he could open the window, and the rest would be plain sailing.

Unhappily, there was one flaw in his scheme. He had conceived that scheme in the expectation that the window would be as he had left it.

But it was not.

During his absence somebody had shot the bolt. And, try his hardest, he could not move the sash an inch.

XVII

FENN HUNTS FOR HIMSELF

Nobody knows for certain the feelings of the camel when his proprietor placed that last straw on his back. The incident happened so long ago. If it had occurred in modern times, he would probably have contributed a first-hand report to the Daily Mail. But it is very likely that he felt on that occasion exactly as Fenn felt when, after a night of unparalleled misadventure, he found that somebody had cut off his retreat by latching the window. After a gruelling race Fate had just beaten him on the tape.

There was no doubt about its being latched. The sash had not merely stuck. He put all he knew into the effort to raise it, but without a hint of success. After three attempts he climbed down again and, sitting on the garden-seat, began to review his position.

If one has an active mind and a fair degree of optimism, the effect of the "staggerers" administered by Fate passes off after a while. Fenn had both. The consequence was that, after ten minutes of grey despair, he was relieved by a faint hope that there might be some other way into the house than through his study. Anyhow, it would be worth while to investigate.

His study was at the side of the house. At the back were the kitchen, the scullery, and the dining-room, and above these more studies and a couple of dormitories. As a last resort he might fling rocks and other solids at the windows until he woke somebody up. But he did not feel like trying this plan until every other had failed. He had no desire to let a garrulous dormitory into the secret of his wanderings. What he hoped was that he might find one of the lower windows open.

And so he did.

As he turned the corner of the house he saw what he had been looking for. The very first window was wide open. His spirits shot up, and for the first time since he had left the theatre he was conscious of taking a pleasure in his adventurous career. Fate was with him after all. He could not help smiling as he remembered how he had felt during that ten minutes on the garden-seat, when the future seemed blank and devoid of any comfort whatsoever. And all the time he could have got in without an effort, if he had only thought of walking half a dozen yards.

Now that the way was open to him, he wasted no time. He climbed through into the dark room. He was not certain which room it was, in spite of his lengthy residence at Kay's.

He let himself down softly till his foot touched the floor. After a moment's pause he moved forward a step. Then another. At the third step his knee struck the leg of a table. He must be in the dining-room. If so, he was all right. He could find his way up to his room with his eyes shut. It was easy to find out for certain. The walls of the dining-room at Kay's, as in the other houses, were covered with photographs. He walked gingerly in the direction in which he imagined the nearest wall to be, reached it, and passed his hand along it. Yes, there were photographs. Then all he had to do was to find the table again, make his way along it, and when he got to the end the door would be a yard or so to his left. The programme seemed simple and attractive. But it was added to in a manner which he had not foreseen. Feeling his way back to the table, he upset a chair. If he had upset a cart-load of coal on to a sheet of tin it could not, so it seemed to him in the disordered state of his nerves, have made more noise. It went down with an appalling crash, striking the table on its way. "This," thought Fenn, savagely, as he waited, listening, "is where I get collared. What a fool I am to barge about like this."

He felt that the echoes of that crash must have penetrated to every corner of the house. But no one came. Perhaps, after all, the noise had not been so great. He proceeded on his journey down the table, feeling every inch of the way. The place seemed one bristling mass of chairs. But, by the exercise of consummate caution, he upset no more and won through at last in safety to the door.

It was at this point that the really lively and exciting part of his adventure began. Compared with what was to follow, his evening had been up to the present dull and monotonous.

As he opened the door there was a sudden stir and crash at the other end of the room. Fenn had upset one chair and the noise had nearly deafened him. Now chairs seemed to be falling in dozens.

93

Bang! Bang! Crash!! (two that time). And then somebody shot through the window like a harlequin and dashed away across the lawn. Fenn could hear his footsteps thudding on the soft turf. And at the same moment other footsteps made themselves heard.

Somebody was coming downstairs.

"Who is that? Is anybody there?"

It was Mr Kay's voice, unmistakably nervous. Fenn darted from the door and across the passage. At the other side was a boot-cupboard. It was his only refuge in that direction. What he ought to have done was to leave the dining-room by the opposite door, which led via a corridor to the junior dayroom. But he lost his head, and instead of bolting away from the enemy, went towards him.

The stairs down which Mr Kay was approaching were at the end of the passage. To reach the dining-room one turned to the right. Beyond the stairs on the left the passage ended in a wall, so that Mr Kay was bound to take the right direction in the search. Fenn wondered if he had a pistol. Not that he cared very much. If the house-master was going to find him, it would be very little extra discomfort to be shot at. And Mr Kay's talents as a marksman were in all probability limited to picking off sitting haystacks. The important point was that he had a candle. A faint yellow glow preceded him down the stairs. Playing hide-and-seek with him in the dark, Fenn might have slipped past in safety; but the candle made that impossible.

He found the boot-room door and slipped through just as Mr Kay turned the corner. With a thrill of pleasure he found that there was a key inside. He turned it as quietly as he could, but nevertheless it grated. Having done this, and seeing nothing else that he could do except await developments, he sat down on the floor among the boots. It was not a dignified position for a man who had played for his county while still at school, but just then he would not have exchanged it for a throne—if the throne had been placed in the passage or the dining-room.

The only question was—had he been seen or heard? He thought not; but his heart began to beat furiously as the footsteps stopped outside the cupboard door and unseen fingers rattled the handle.

Twice Mr Kay tried the handle, but, finding the cupboard locked, passed on into the dining-room. The light of the candle ceased to shine under the door, and Fenn was once more in inky darkness.

He listened intently. A minute later he had made his second mistake. Instead of waiting, as he should have done, until Mr Kay had retired for good, he unlocked the door directly he had passed, and when a muffled crash told him that the house-master was in the dining-room among the chairs, out he came and fled softly upstairs towards his bedroom. He thought that Mr Kay might possibly take it into his head to go round the dormitories to make certain that all the members of his house were in. In which case all would be discovered.

When he reached his room he began to fling off his clothes with feverish haste. Once in bed all would be well.

He had got out of his boots, his coat, and his waistcoat, and was beginning to feel that electric sensation of triumph which only conies to the man who just pulls through, when he heard Mr Kay coming down the corridor towards his room. The burglar-hunter, returning from the dining-room in the full belief that the miscreant had escaped through the open window, had had all his ardour for the chase redoubled by the sight of the cupboard door, which Fenn in his hurry had not remembered to close. Mr Kay had made certain by two separate trials that that door had been locked. And now it was wide open. Ergo, the apostle of the jemmy and the skeleton key must still be in the house. Mr Kay, secure in the recollection that burglars never show fight if they can possibly help it, determined to search the house.

Fenn made up his mind swiftly. There was no time to finish dressing. Mr Kay, peering round, might note the absence of the rest of his clothes from their accustomed pegs if he got into bed as he was. There was only one thing to be done. He threw back the bed-clothes, ruffled the sheets till the bed looked as if it had been slept in, and opened the door just as Mr Kay reached the threshold.

"Anything the matter, sir?" asked Fenn, promptly. "I heard a noise downstairs. Can I help you?"

Mr Kay looked carefully at the ex-head of his house. Fenn was a finely-developed youth. He stood six feet, and all of him that was not bone was muscle. A useful colleague to have by one in a hunt for a possibly ferocious burglar.

So thought Mr Kay.

"So you heard the noise?" he said. "Well, perhaps you had better come with me. There is no doubt that a burglar has entered the house tonight, in spite of the fact that I locked all the windows myself. Your study window was unlocked, Fenn. It was extremely careless of you to leave it in such a condition, and I hope you will be more careful in future. Why, somebody might have got in through it."

Fenn thought it was not at all unlikely.

"Come along, then. I am sure the man is still in the house. He was hiding in the cupboard by the dining-room. I know it. I am sure he is still in the house."

But, in spite of the fact that Fenn was equally sure, half an hour's search failed to discover any lurking evil-doer.

"You had better go to bed, Fenn," said Mr Kay, disgustedly, at the end of that period. "He must have got back in some extraordinary manner."

"Yes, sir," agreed Fenn.

He himself had certainly got back in a very extraordinary manner.

However, he had got back, which was the main point.

XVIII

A VAIN QUEST

After all he had gone through that night, it disturbed Fenn very little to find on the following morning that the professional cracksman had gone off with one of the cups in his study. Certainly, it was not as bad as it might have been, for he had only abstracted one out of the half dozen that decorated the room. Fenn was a fine runner, and had won the "sprint" events at the sports for two years now.

The news of the burglary at Kay's soon spread about the school. Mr Kay mentioned it to Mr Mulholland, and Mr Mulholland discussed it at lunch with the prefects of his house. The juniors of Kay's were among the last to hear of it, but when they did, they made the most of it, to the disgust of the School House fags, to whom the episode seemed in the nature of an infringement of copyright. Several spirited by-battles took place that day owing to this, and at the lower end of the table of Kay's dining-room at tea that evening there could be seen many swollen countenances. All, however, wore pleased smiles. They had proved to the School House their right to have a burglary of their own if they liked. It was the first occasion since Kennedy had become head of the house that Kay's had united in a common and patriotic cause.

Directly afternoon school was over that day, Fenn started for the town. The only thing that caused him any anxiety now was the fear lest the cap which he had left in the house in the High Street might rise up as evidence against him later on. Except for that, he was safe. The headmaster had evidently not remembered his absence from the festive board, or he would have spoken to him on the subject before now. If he could but recover the lost cap, all would be right with the world. Give him back that cap, and he would turn over a new leaf with a rapidity and emphasis which would lower the world's record for that performance. He would be a reformed character. He would even go to the extent of calling a truce with Mr Kay, climbing down to Kennedy, and offering him his services in his attempt to lick the house into shape.

As a matter of fact, he had had this idea before. Jimmy Silver, who was in the position—common at school—of being very friendly with two people who were not on speaking terms, had been at him on the topic.

"It's rot," James had said, with perfect truth, "to see two chaps like you making idiots of themselves over a house like Kay's. And it's all your fault, too," he had added frankly. "You know jolly well you aren't playing the game. You ought to be backing Kennedy up all the time. Instead of which, you go about trying to look like a Christian martyr—"

"I don't," said Fenn, indignantly.

"Well, like a stuffed frog, then—it's all the same to me. It's perfect rot. If I'm walking with Kennedy, you stalk past as if we'd both got the plague or something. And if I'm with you, Kennedy suddenly remembers an appointment, and dashes off at a gallop in the opposite direction. If I had to award the bronze medal for drivelling lunacy in this place, you would get it by a narrow margin, and Kennedy would be proxime, and honourably mentioned. Silly idiots!"

"Don't stop, Jimmy. Keep it up," said Fenn, settling himself in his chair. The dialogue was taking place in Silver's study.

"My dear chap, you didn't think I'd finished, surely! I was only trying to find some description that would suit you. But it's no good. I can't. Look here, take my advice—the advice," he added, in the melodramatic voice he was in the habit of using whenever he wished to conceal the fact that he was speaking seriously, "of an old man who wishes ye both well. Go to Kennedy, fling yourself on his chest, and say, 'We have done those things which we ought not to have done—' No. As you were! Compn'y, 'shun! Say 'J. Silver says that I am a rotter. I am a worm. I have made an ass of myself. But I will be good. Shake, pard!' That's what you've got to do. Come in."

And in had come Kennedy. The attractions of Kay's were small, and he usually looked in on Jimmy Silver in the afternoons.

"Oh, sorry," he said, as he saw Fenn. "I thought you were alone, Jimmy."

"I was just going," said Fenn, politely.

"Oh, don't let me disturb you," protested Kennedy, with winning courtesy.

"Not at all," said Fenn.

"Oh, if you really were—"

"Oh, yes, really."

"Get out, then," growled Jimmy, who had been listening in speechless disgust to the beautifully polite conversation just recorded. "I'll forward that bronze medal to you, Fenn."

And as the door closed he had turned to rend Kennedy as he had rent Fenn; while Fenn walked back to Kay's feeling that there was a good deal in what Jimmy had said.

So that when he went down town that afternoon in search of his cap, he pondered as he walked over the advisability of making a fresh start. It would not be a bad idea. But first he must concentrate his energies on recovering what he had lost.

He found the house in the High Street without a great deal of difficulty, for he had marked the spot carefully as far as that had been possible in the fog.

The door was opened to him, not by the old man with whom he had exchanged amenities on the previous night, but by a short, thick fellow, who looked exactly like a picture of a loafer from the pages of a comic journal. He eyed Fenn with what might have been meant for an inquiring look. To Fenn it seemed merely menacing.

"Wodyer want?" he asked, abruptly.

Eckleton was not a great distance from London, and, as a consequence, many of London's choicest blackguards migrated there from time to time. During the hopping season, and while the local races were on, one might meet with two Cockney twangs for every country accent.

"I want to see the old gentleman who lives here," said Fenn.

"Wot old gentleman?"

"I'm afraid I don't know his name. Is this a home for old gentlemen? If you'll bring out all you've got, I'll find my one."

"Wodyer want see the old gentleman for?"

99

"To ask for my cap. I left it here last night."

"Oh, yer left it 'ere last night! Well, yer cawn't see 'im."

"Not from here, no," agreed Fenn. "Being only eyes, you see," he quoted happily, "my wision's limited. But if you wouldn't mind moving out of the way—"

"Yer cawn't see 'im. Blimey, 'ow much more of it, I should like to know. Gerroutovit, cawn't yer! You and yer caps."

And he added a searching expletive by way of concluding the sentence fittingly. After which he slipped back and slammed the door, leaving Fenn waiting outside like the Peri at the gate of Paradise.

His resemblance to the Peri ceased after the first quarter of a minute. That lady, we read, took her expulsion lying down. Fenn was more vigorous. He seized the knocker, and banged lustily on the door. He had given up all hope of getting back the cap. All he wanted was to get the doorkeeper out into the open again, when he would proceed to show him, to the best of his ability, what was what. It would not be the first time he had taken on a gentleman of the same class and a similar type of conversation.

But the man refused to be drawn. For all the reply Fenn's knocking produced, the house might have been empty. At last, having tired his wrist and collected a small crowd of Young Eckleton, who looked as if they expected him to proceed to further efforts for their amusement, he gave it up, and retired down the High Street with what dignity he could command—which, as he was followed for the first fifty yards by the silent but obviously expectant youths, was not a great deal.

They left him, disappointed, near the Town Hall, and Fenn continued on his way alone. The window of the grocer's shop, with its tins of preserved apricots and pots of jam, recalled to his mind what he had forgotten, that the food at Kay's, though it might be wholesome (which he doubted), was undeniably plain, and, secondly, that he had run out of jam. Now that he was here he might as well supply that deficiency.

Now it chanced that Master Wren, of Kay's, was down town—without leave, as was his habit—on an errand of a very similar

100

nature. Walton had found that he, like Fenn, lacked those luxuries of life which are so much more necessary than necessities, and, being unable to go himself, owing to the unfortunate accident of being kept in by his form-master, had asked Wren to go for him. Wren's visit to the grocer's was just ending when Fenn's began.

They met in the doorway.

Wren looked embarrassed, and nearly dropped a pot of honey, which he secured low down after the manner of a catch in the slips. Fenn, on the other hand, took no notice of his fellow-Kayite, but walked on into the shop and began to inspect the tins of biscuits which were stacked on the floor by the counter.

XIX

THE GUILE OF WREN

Wren did not quite know what to make of this. Why had not Fenn said a word to him? There were one or two prefects in the school whom he might have met even at such close quarters and yet have cherished a hope that they had not seen him. Once he had run right into Drew, of the School House, and escaped unrecognised. But with Fenn it was different. Compared to Fenn, lynxes were astigmatic. He must have spotted him.

There was a vein of philosophy in Wren's composition. He felt that he might just as well be hanged for a sheep as a lamb. In other words, having been caught down town without leave, he might as well stay there and enjoy himself a little while longer before going back to be executed. So he strolled off down the High Street, bought a few things at a stationer's, and wound up with an excellent tea at the confectioner's by the post-office.

It was as he was going to this meal that Kennedy caught sight of him. Kennedy had come down town to visit the local photographer, to whom he had entrusted a fortnight before the pleasant task of taking his photograph. As he had heard nothing from him since, he was now coming to investigate. He entered the High Street as Wren was turning into the confectioner's, saw him, and made a note of it for future reference.

When Wren returned to the house just before lock-up, he sought counsel of Walton.

"I say," he said, as he handed over the honey he had saved so neatly from destruction, "what would you do? Just as I was coming out of the shop, I barged into Fenn. He must have twigged me."

"Didn't he say anything?"

"Not a word. I couldn't make it out, because he must have seen me. We weren't a yard away from one another."

"It's dark in the shop," suggested Walton.

"Not at the door; which is where we met."

Before Walton could find anything to say in reply to this, their conversation was interrupted by Spencer.

"Kennedy wants you, Wren," said Spencer. "You'd better buck up; he's in an awful wax."

Next to Walton, the vindictive Spencer objected most to Wren, and he did not attempt to conceal the pleasure he felt in being the bearer of this ominous summons.

The group broke up. Wren went disconsolately upstairs to Kennedy's study; Walton smacked Spencer's head—more as a matter of form than because he had done anything special to annoy him—and retired to the senior dayroom; while Spencer, muttering darkly to himself, avoided a second smack and took cover in the junior room, where he consoled himself by toasting a piece of india-rubber in the gas till it made the atmosphere painful to breathe in, and recalling with pleasure the condition Walton's face had been in for the day or two following his encounter with Kennedy in the dormitory.

Kennedy was working when Wren knocked at his door.

He had not much time to spare on a bounds-breaking fag; and his manner was curt.

"I saw you going into Rose's, in the High Street, this afternoon, Wren," he said, looking up from his Greek prose. "I didn't give you leave. Come up here after prayers tonight. Shut the door."

Wren went down to consult Walton again. His attitude with regard to a licking from the head of the house was much like that of the other fags. Custom had, to a certain extent, inured him to these painful interviews, but still, if it was possible, he preferred to keep out of them. Under Fenn's rule he had often found a tolerably thin excuse serve his need. Fenn had so many other things to do that he was not unwilling to forego an occasional licking, if the excuse was good enough. And he never took the trouble to find out whether the ingenious stories Wren was wont to serve up to him were true or not. Kennedy, Wren reflected uncomfortably, had given signs that this easy-going method would not do for him. Still, it might be possible to hunt up some story that would meet the case. Walton had a gift in that direction.

"He says I'm to go to his study after prayers," reported Wren. "Can't you think of any excuse that would do?"

"Can't understand Fenn running you in," said Walton. "I thought he never spoke to Kennedy."

Wren explained.

"It wasn't Fenn who ran me in. Kennedy was down town, too, and twigged me going into Rose's. I went there and had tea after I got your things at the grocer's."

"Oh, he spotted you himself, did he?" said Walton. "And he doesn't know Fenn saw you?"

"I don't think so."

"Then I've got a ripping idea. When he has you up tonight, swear that you got leave from Fenn to go down town."

"But he'll ask him."

"The odds are that he won't. He and Fenn had a row at the beginning of term, and never speak to one another if they can help it. It's ten to one that he will prefer taking your yarn to going and asking Fenn if it's true or not. Then he's bound to let you off."

Wren admitted that the scheme was sound.

At the conclusion of prayers, therefore, he went up again to Kennedy's study, with a more hopeful air than he had worn on his previous visit.

"Come in," said Kennedy, reaching for the swagger-stick which he was accustomed to use at these ceremonies.

"Please, Kennedy," said Wren, glibly. "I did get leave to go down town this afternoon."

"What!"

Wren repeated the assertion.

"Who gave you leave?"

"Fenn."

104

The thing did not seem to be working properly. When he said the word "Fenn", Wren expected to see Kennedy retire baffled, conscious that there was nothing more to be said or done. Instead of this, the remark appeared to infuriate him.

"It's just like your beastly cheek," he said, glaring at the red-headed delinquent, "to ask Fenn for leave instead of me. You know perfectly well that only the head of the house can give leave to go down town. I don't know how often you and the rest of the junior dayroom have played this game, but it's going to stop now. You'd better remember another time when you want to go to Rose's that I've got to be consulted first."

With which he proceeded to ensure to the best of his ability that the memory of Master Wren should not again prove treacherous in this respect.

"How did it work?" asked Walton, when Wren returned.

"It didn't," said Wren, briefly.

Walton expressed an opinion that Kennedy was a cad; which, however sound in itself, did little to improve the condition of Wren.

Having disposed of Wren, Kennedy sat down seriously to consider this new development of a difficult situation. Hitherto he had imagined Fenn to be merely a sort of passive resister who confined himself to the Achilles-in-his-tent business, and was only a nuisance because he refused to back him up. To find him actually aiding and abetting the house in its opposition to its head was something of a shock. And yet, if he had given Wren leave to go down town, he had probably done the same kind office by others. It irritated Kennedy more than the most overt act of enmity would have done. It was not good form. It was hitting below the belt. There was, of course, the chance that Wren's story had not been true. But he did not build much on that. He did not yet know his Wren well, and believed that such an audacious lie would be beyond the daring of a fag. But it would be worth while to make inquiries. He went down the passage to Fenn's study. Fenn, however, had gone to bed, so he resolved to approach him on the subject next day. There was no hurry.

He went to his dormitory, feeling very bitter towards Fenn, and rehearsing home truths with which to confound him on the morrow.

XX

JIMMY THE PEACEMAKER

In these hustling times it is not always easy to get ten minutes' conversation with an acquaintance in private. There was drill in the dinner hour next day for the corps, to which Kennedy had to go directly after lunch. It did not end till afternoon school began. When afternoon school was over, he had to turn out and practise scrummaging with the first fifteen, in view of an important school match which was coming off on the following Saturday. Kennedy had not yet received his cap, but he was playing regularly for the first fifteen, and was generally looked upon as a certainty for one of the last places in the team. Fenn, being a three-quarter, had not to participate in this practice. While the forwards were scrummaging on the second fifteen ground, the outsides ran and passed on the first fifteen ground over at the other end of the field. Fenn's training for the day finished earlier than Kennedy's, the captain of the Eckleton fifteen, who led the scrum, not being satisfied with the way in which the forwards wheeled. He kept them for a quarter of an hour after the outsides had done their day's work, and when Kennedy got back to the house and went to Fenn's study, the latter was not there. He had evidently changed and gone out again, for his football clothes were lying in a heap in a corner of the room. Going back to his own study, he met Spencer.

"Have you seen Fenn?" he asked.

"No," said the fag. "He hasn't come in."

"He's come in all right, but he's gone out again. Go and ask Taylor if he knows where he is."

Taylor was Fenn's fag.

Spencer went to the junior dayroom, and returned with the information that Taylor did not know.

"Oh, all right, then—it doesn't matter," said Kennedy, and went into his study to change.

He had completed this operation, and was thinking of putting his kettle on for tea, when there was a knock at the door.

It was Baker, Jimmy Silver's fag.

"Oh, Kennedy," he said, "Silver says, if you aren't doing anything special, will you go over to his study to tea?"

"Why, is there anything on?"

It struck him as curious that Jimmy should take the trouble to send his fag over to Kay's with a formal invitation. As a rule the head of Blackburn's kept open house. His friends were given to understand that they could drop in whenever they liked. Kennedy looked in for tea three times a week on an average.

"I don't think so," said Baker.

"Who else is going to be there?"

Jimmy Silver sometimes took it into his head to entertain weird beings from other houses whose brothers or cousins he had met in the holidays. On such occasions he liked to have some trusty friend by him to help the conversation along. It struck Kennedy that this might be one of those occasions. If so, he would send back a polite but firm refusal of the invitation. Last time he had gone to help Jimmy entertain a guest of this kind, conversation had come to a dead standstill a quarter of an hour after his arrival, the guest refusing to do anything except eat prodigiously, and reply "Yes" or "No", as the question might demand, when spoken to. Also he had declined to stir from his seat till a quarter to seven. Kennedy was not going to be let in for another orgy of that nature if he knew it.

"Who's with Silver?" he asked.

"Only Fenn," said Baker.

Kennedy pondered for a moment.

"All right," he said, at last, "tell him I'll be round in a few minutes."

He sat thinking the thing over after Baker had gone back to Blackburn's with the message. He saw Silver's game, of course. Jimmy had made no secret for some time of his disgust at the coolness between Kennedy and Fenn. Not knowing all the

107

circumstances, he considered it absolute folly. If only he could get the two together over a quiet pot of tea, he imagined that it would not be a difficult task to act effectively as a peacemaker.

Kennedy was sorry for Jimmy. He appreciated his feelings in the matter. He would not have liked it himself if his two best friends had been at daggers drawn. Still, he could not bring himself to treat Fenn as if nothing had happened, simply to oblige Silver. There had been a time when he might have done it, but now that Fenn had started a deliberate campaign against him by giving Wren—and probably, thought Kennedy, half the other fags in the house—leave down town when he ought to have sent them on to him, things had gone too far. However, he could do no harm by going over to Jimmy's to tea, even if Fenn was there. He had not looked to interview Fenn before an audience, but if that audience consisted only of Jimmy, it would not matter so much.

His advent surprised Fenn. The astute James, fancying that if he mentioned that he was expecting Kennedy to tea, Fenn would make a bolt for it, had said nothing about it.

When Kennedy arrived there was one of those awkward pauses which are so difficult to fill up in a satisfactory manner.

"Now you're up, Fenn," said Jimmy, as the latter rose, evidently with the intention of leaving the study, "you might as well reach down that toasting-fork and make some toast."

"I'm afraid I must be off now, Jimmy," said Fenn.

"No you aren't," said Silver. "You bustle about and make yourself useful, and don't talk rot. You'll find your cup on that shelf over there, Kennedy. It'll want a wipe round. Better use the table-cloth."

There was silence in the study until tea was ready. Then Jimmy Silver spoke.

"Long time since we three had tea together," he said, addressing the remark to the teapot.

"Kennedy's a busy man," said Fenn, suavely. "He's got a house to look after."

"And I'm going to look after it," said Kennedy, "as you'll find."

Jimmy Silver put in a plaintive protest.

"I wish you two men wouldn't talk shop," he said. "It's bad enough having Kay's next door to one, without your dragging it into the conversation. How were the forwards this evening, Kennedy?"

"Not bad," said Kennedy, shortly.

"I wonder if we shall lick Tuppenham on Saturday?"

"I don't know," said Kennedy; and there was silence again.

"Look here, Jimmy," said Kennedy, after a long pause, during which the head of Blackburn's tried to fill up the blank in the conversation by toasting a piece of bread in a way which was intended to suggest that if he were not so busy, the talk would be unchecked and animated, "it's no good. We must have it out some time, so it may as well be here as anywhere else. I've been looking for Fenn all day."

"Sorry to give you all that trouble," said Fenn, with a sneer. "Got something important to say?"

"Yes."

"Go ahead, then."

Jimmy Silver stood between them with the toasting-fork in his hand, as if he meant to plunge it into the one who first showed symptoms of flying at the other's throat. He was unhappy. His peace-making tea-party was not proving a success.

"I wanted to ask you," said Kennedy, quietly, "what you meant by giving the fags leave down town when you knew that they ought to come to me?"

The gentle and intelligent reader will remember (though that miserable worm, the vapid and irreflective reader, will have forgotten) that at the beginning of the term the fags of Kay's had endeavoured to show their approval of Fenn and their disapproval of Kennedy by applying to the former for leave when they wished to go to the town; and that Fenn had received them in the most ungrateful manner with blows instead of exeats. Strong in this recollection, he was not disturbed by Kennedy's question. Indeed, it gave him a comfortable feeling of rectitude. There is nothing more pleasant than to be accused to your face of something which you can deny on the spot with an easy conscience. It is like getting a very loose ball at cricket. Fenn felt almost friendly towards Kennedy.

109

"I meant nothing," he replied, "for the simple reason that I didn't do it."

"I caught Wren down town yesterday, and he said you had given him leave."

"Then he lied, and I hope you licked him."

"There you are, you see," broke in Jimmy Silver triumphantly, "it's all a misunderstanding. You two have got no right to be cutting one another. Why on earth can't you stop all this rot, and behave like decent members of society again?"

"As a matter of fact," said Fenn, "they did try it on earlier in the term. I wasted a lot of valuable time pointing out to them with a swagger-stick—that I was the wrong person to come to. I'm sorry you should have thought I could play it as low down as that."

Kennedy hesitated. It is not very pleasant to have to climb down after starting a conversation in a stormy and wrathful vein. But it had to be done.

"I'm sorry, Fenn," he said; "I was an idiot."

Jimmy Silver cut in again.

"You were," he said, with enthusiasm. "You both were. I used to think Fenn was a bigger idiot than you, but now I'm inclined to call it a dead heat. What's the good of going on trying to see which of you can make the bigger fool of himself? You've both lowered all previous records."

"I suppose we have," said Fenn. "At least, I have."

"No, I have," said Kennedy.

"You both have," said Jimmy Silver. "Another cup of tea, anybody? Say when."

Fenn and Kennedy walked back to Kay's together, and tea-d together in Fenn's study on the following afternoon, to the amazement—and even scandal—of Master Spencer, who discovered them at it. Spencer liked excitement; and with the two leaders of the house at logger-heads, things could never be really dull. If, as appearances seemed to suggest, they had agreed to settle their differences, life would become monotonous again—possibly even unpleasant.

This thought flashed through Spencer's brain (as he called it) when he opened Fenn's door and found him helping Kennedy to tea.

"Oh, the headmaster wants to see you, please, Fenn," said Spencer, recovering from his amazement, "and told me to give you this."

"This" was a prefect's cap. Fenn recognised it without difficulty. It was the cap he had left in the sitting-room of the house in the High Street.

XXI

IN WHICH AN EPISODE IS CLOSED

"Thanks," said Fenn.

He stood twirling the cap round in his hand as Spencer closed the door. Then he threw it on to the table. He did not feel particularly disturbed at the thought of the interview that was to come. He had been expecting the cap to turn up, like the corpse of Eugene Aram's victim, at some inconvenient moment. It was a pity that it had come just as things looked as if they might be made more or less tolerable in Kay's. He had been looking forward with a grim pleasure to the sensation that would be caused in the house when it became known that he and Kennedy had formed a combine for its moral and physical benefit. But that was all over. He would be sacked, beyond a doubt. In the history of Eckleton, as far as he knew it, there had never been a case of a fellow breaking out at night and not being expelled when he was caught. It was one of the cardinal sins in the school code. There had been the case of Peter Brown, which his brother had mentioned in his letter. And in his own time he had seen three men vanish from Eckleton for the same offence. He did not flatter himself that his record at the school was so good as to make it likely that the authorities would stretch a point in his favour.

"So long, Kennedy," he said. "You'll be here when I get back, I suppose?"

"What does he want you for, do you think?" asked Kennedy, stretching himself, with a yawn. It never struck him that Fenn could be in any serious trouble. Fenn was a prefect; and when the headmaster sent for a prefect, it was generally to tell him that he had got a split infinitive in his English Essay that week.

"Glad I'm not you," he added, as a gust of wind rattled the sash, and the rain dashed against the pane. "Beastly evening to have to go out."

"It isn't the rain I mind," said Fenn; "it's what's going to happen when I get indoors again," and refused to explain further. There would be plenty of time to tell Kennedy the whole story when he returned. It was better not to keep the headmaster waiting.

The first thing he noticed on reaching the School House was the strange demeanour of the butler. Whenever Fenn had had occasion to call on the headmaster hitherto, Watson had admitted him with the air of a high priest leading a devotee to a shrine of which he was the sole managing director. This evening he seemed restless, excited.

"Good evening, Mr Fenn," he said. "This way, sir."

Those were his actual words. Fenn had not known for certain until now that he could talk. On previous occasions their conversations had been limited to an "Is the headmaster in?" from Fenn, and a stately inclination of the head from Watson. The man was getting a positive babbler.

With an eager, springy step, distantly reminiscent of a shopwalker heading a procession of customers, with a touch of the style of the winner in a walking-race to Brighton, the once slow-moving butler led the way to the headmaster's study.

For the first time since he started out, Fenn was conscious of a tremor. There is something about a closed door, behind which somebody is waiting to receive one, which appeals to the imagination, especially if the ensuing meeting is likely to be an unpleasant one.

"Ah, Fenn," said the headmaster. "Come in."

Fenn wondered. It was not in this tone of voice that the Head was wont to begin a conversation which was going to prove painful.

"You've got your cap, Fenn? I gave it to a small boy in your house to take to you."

"Yes, sir."

He had given up all hope of understanding the Head's line of action. Unless he was playing a deep game, and intended to flash out suddenly with a keen question which it would be impossible to parry, there seemed nothing to account for the strange absence of anything unusual in his manner. He referred to the cap as if he had

113

borrowed it from Fenn, and had returned it by bearer, hoping that its loss had not inconvenienced him at all.

"I daresay," continued the Head, "that you are wondering how it came into my possession. You missed it, of course?"

"Very much, sir," said Fenn, with perfect truth.

"It has just been brought to my house, together with a great many other things, more valuable, perhaps,"—here he smiled a head-magisterial smile—"by a policeman from Eckleton."

Fenn was still unequal to the intellectual pressure of the conversation. He could understand, in a vague way, that for some unexplained reason things were going well for him, but beyond that his mind was in a whirl.

"You will remember the unfortunate burglary of Mr Kay's house and mine. Your cap was returned with the rest of the stolen property."

"Just so," thought Fenn. "The rest of the stolen property? Exactly. Go on. Don't mind me. I shall begin to understand soon, I suppose."

He condensed these thoughts into the verbal reply, "Yes, sir."

"I sent for you to identify your own property. I see there is a silver cup belonging to you. Perhaps there are also other articles. Go and see. You will find them on that table. They are in a hopeless state of confusion, having been conveyed here in a sack. Fortunately, nothing is broken."

He was thinking of certain valuables belonging to himself which had been abstracted from his drawing-room on the occasion of the burglar's visit to the School House.

Fenn crossed the room, and began to inspect the table indicated. On it was as mixed a collection of valuable and useless articles as one could wish to see. He saw his cup at once, and attached himself to it. But of all the other exhibits in this private collection, he could recognise nothing else as his property.

"There is nothing of mine here except the cup, sir," he said.

"Ah. Then that is all, I think. You are going back to Mr Kay's. Then please send Kennedy to me. Good night, Fenn."

114

"Good night, sir."

Even now Fenn could not understand it. The more he thought it over, the more his brain reeled. He could grasp the fact that his cap and his cup were safe again, and that there was evidently going to be no sacking for the moment. But how it had all happened, and how the police had got hold of his cap, and why they had returned it with the loot gathered in by the burglar who had visited Kay's and the School House, were problems which, he had to confess, were beyond him.

He walked to Kay's through the rain with the cup under his mackintosh, and freely admitted to himself that there were things in heaven and earth—and particularly earth—which no fellow could understand.

"I don't know," he said, when Kennedy pressed for an explanation of the reappearance of the cup. "It's no good asking me. I'm going now to borrow the matron's smelling-salts: I feel faint. After that I shall wrap a wet towel round my head, and begin to think it out. Meanwhile, you're to go over to the Head. He's had enough of me, and he wants to have a look at you."

"Me?" said Kennedy. "Why?"

"Now, is it any good asking me??" said Fenn. "If you can find out what it's all about, I'll thank you if you'll come and tell me."

Ten minutes later Kennedy returned. He carried a watch and chain.

"I couldn't think what had happened to my watch," he said. "I missed it on the day after that burglary here, but I never thought of thinking it had been collared by a professional. I thought I must have lost it somewhere."

"Well, have you grasped what's been happening?"

"I've grasped my ticker, which is good enough for me. Half a second. The old man wants to see the rest of the prefects. He's going to work through the house in batches, instead of man by man. I'll just go round the studies and rout them out, and then I'll come back and explain. It's perfectly simple."

"Glad you think so," said Fenn.

Kennedy went and returned.

115

"Now," he said, subsiding into a deck-chair, "what is it you don't understand?"

"I don't understand anything. Begin at the beginning."

"I got the yarn from the butler—what's his name?"

"Those who know him well enough to venture to give him a name— I've never dared to myself—call him Watson," said Fenn.

"I got the yarn from Watson. He was as excited as anything about it. I never saw him like that before."

"I noticed something queer about him."

"He's awfully bucked, and is doing the Ancient Mariner business all over the place. Wants to tell the story to everyone he sees."

"Well, suppose you follow his example. I want to hear about it."

"Well, it seems that the police have been watching a house at the corner of the High Street for some time—what's up?"

"Nothing. Go on."

"But you said, 'By Jove!'"

"Well, why shouldn't I say 'By Jove'? When you are telling sensational yarns, it's my duty to say something of the sort. Buck along."

"It's a house not far from the Town Hall, at the corner of Pegwell Street—you've probably been there scores of times."

"Once or twice, perhaps," said Fenn. "Well?"

"About a month ago two suspicious-looking bounders went to live there. Watson says their faces were enough to hang them. Anyhow, they must have been pretty bad, for they made even the Eckleton police, who are pretty average-sized rotters, suspicious, and they kept an eye on them. Well, after a bit there began to be a regular epidemic of burglary round about here. Watson says half the houses round were broken into. The police thought it was getting a bit too thick, but they didn't like to raid the house without some jolly good evidence that these two men were the burglars, so they lay low and waited till they should give them a decent excuse for jumping on

116

them. They had had a detective chap down from London, by the way, to see if he couldn't do something about the burglaries, and he kept his eye on them, too."

"They had quite a gallery. Didn't they notice any of the eyes?"

"No. Then after a bit one of them nipped off to London with a big bag. The detective chap was after him like a shot. He followed him from the station, saw him get into a cab, got into another himself, and stuck to him hard. The front cab stopped at about a dozen pawnbrokers' shops. The detective Johnny took the names and addresses, and hung on to the burglar man all day, and finally saw him return to the station, where he caught a train back to Eckleton. Directly he had seen him off, the detective got into a cab, called on the dozen pawnbrokers, showed his card, with 'Scotland Yard' on it, I suppose, and asked to see what the other chap had pawned. He identified every single thing as something that had been collared from one of the houses round Eckleton way. So he came back here, told the police, and they raided the house, and there they found stacks of loot of all descriptions."

"Including my cap," said Fenn, thoughtfully. "I see now."

"Rummy the man thinking it worth his while to take an old cap," said Kennedy.

"Very," said Fenn. "But it's been a rum business all along."

117

XXII

KAY'S CHANGES ITS NAME

For the remaining weeks of the winter term, things went as smoothly in Kay's as Kay would let them. That restless gentleman still continued to burst in on Kennedy from time to time with some sensational story of how he had found a fag doing what he ought not to have done. But there was a world of difference between the effect these visits had now and that which they had had when Kennedy had stood alone in the house, his hand against all men. Now that he could work off the effects of such encounters by going straight to Fenn's study and picking the house-master to pieces, the latter's peculiar methods ceased to be irritating, and became funny. Mr Kay was always ferreting out the weirdest misdoings on the part of the members of his house, and rushing to Kennedy's study to tell him about them at full length, like a rather indignant dog bringing a rat he has hunted down into a drawing-room, to display it to the company. On one occasion, when Fenn and Jimmy Silver were in Kennedy's study, Mr Kay dashed in to complain bitterly that he had discovered that the junior dayroom kept mice in their lockers. Apparently this fact seemed to him enough to cause an epidemic of typhoid fever in the place, and he hauled Kennedy over the coals, in a speech that lasted five minutes, for not having detected this plague-spot in the house.

"So that's the celebrity at home, is it?" said Jimmy Silver, when he had gone. "I now begin to understand more or less why this house wants a new Head every two terms. Is he often taken like that?"

"He's never anything else," said Kennedy. "Fenn keeps a list of the things he rags me about, and we have an even shilling on, each week, that he will beat the record of the previous week. At first I used to get the shilling if he lowered the record; but after a bit it struck us that it wasn't fair, so now we take it on alternate weeks. This is my week, by the way. I think I can trouble you for that bob, Fenn?"

"I wish I could make it more," said Fenn, handing over the shilling.

"What sort of things does he rag you about generally?" inquired Silver.

Fenn produced a slip of paper.

"Here are a few," he said, "for this month. He came in on the 10th because he found two kids fighting. Kennedy was down town when it happened, but that made no difference. Then he caught the senior dayroom making a row of some sort. He said it was perfectly deafening; but we couldn't hear it in our studies. I believe he goes round the house, listening at keyholes. That was on the 16th. On the 22nd he found a chap in Kennedy's dormitory wandering about the house at one in the morning. He seemed to think that Kennedy ought to have sat up all night on the chance of somebody cutting out of the dormitory. At any rate, he ragged him. I won the weekly shilling on that; and deserved it, too."

Fenn had to go over to the gymnasium shortly after this. Jimmy Silver stayed on, talking to Kennedy.

"And bar Kay," said Jimmy, "how do you find the house doing? Any better?"

"Better! It's getting a sort of model establishment. I believe, if we keep pegging away at them, we may win some sort of a cup sooner or later."

"Well, Kay's very nearly won the cricket cup last year. You ought to get it next season, now that you and Fenn are both in the team."

"Oh, I don't know. It'll be a fluke if we do. Still, we're hoping. It isn't every house that's got a county man in it. But we're breaking out in another place. Don't let it get about, for goodness' sake, but we're going for the sports' cup."

"Hope you'll get it. Blackburn's won't have a chance, anyhow, and I should like to see somebody get it away from the School House. They've had it much too long. They're beginning to look on it as their right. But who are your men?"

"Well, Fenn ought to be a cert for the hundred and the quarter, to start with."

"But the School House must get the long run, and the mile, and the half, too, probably."

"Yes. We haven't anyone to beat Milligan, certainly. But there are the second and third places. Don't forget those. That's where we're going to have a look in. There's all sorts of unsuspected talent in Kay's. To look at Peel, for instance, you wouldn't think he could do the hundred in eleven, would you? Well, he can, only he's been too slack to go in for the race at the sports, because it meant training. I had him up here and reasoned with him, and he's promised to do his best. Eleven is good enough for second place in the hundred, don't you think? There are lots of others in the house who can do quite decently on the track, if they try. I've been making strict inquiries. Kay's are hot stuff, Jimmy. Heap big medicine. That's what they are."

"You're a wonderful man, Kennedy," said Jimmy Silver. And he meant it. Kennedy's uphill fight at Kay's had appealed to him strongly. He himself had never known what it meant to have to manage a hostile house. He had stepped into his predecessor's shoes at Blackburn's much as the heir to a throne becomes king. Nobody had thought of disputing his right to the place. He was next man in; so, directly the departure of the previous head of Blackburn's left a vacancy, he stepped into it, and the machinery of the house had gone on as smoothly as if there had been no change at all. But Kennedy had gone in against a slack and antagonistic house, with weak prefects to help him, and a fussy house-master; and he had fought them all for a term, and looked like winning. Jimmy admired his friend with a fervour which nothing on earth would have tempted him to reveal. Like most people with a sense of humour, he had a fear of appearing ridiculous, and he hid his real feelings as completely as he was able.

"How is the footer getting on?" inquired Jimmy, remembering the difficulties Kennedy had encountered earlier in the term in connection with his house team.

"It's better," said Kennedy. "Keener, at any rate. We shall do our best in the house-matches. But we aren't a good team."

"Any more trouble about your being captain instead of Fenn?"

"No. We both sign the lists now. Fenn didn't want to, but I thought it would be a good idea, so we tried it. It seems to have worked all right."

"Of course, your getting your first has probably made a difference."

120

"A bit, perhaps."

"Well, I hope you won't get the footer cup, because I want it for Blackburn's. Or the cricket cup. I want that, too. But you can have the sports' cup with my blessing."

"Thanks," said Kennedy. "It's very generous of you."

"Don't mention it," said Jimmy.

From which conversation it will be seen that Kay's was gradually pulling itself together. It had been asleep for years. It was now waking up.

When the winter term ended, there were distinct symptoms of an outbreak of public spirit in the house.

The Easter term opened auspiciously in one way. Neither Walton nor Perry returned. The former had been snapped up in the middle of the holidays—to his enormous disgust—by a bank, which wanted his services so much that it was prepared to pay him 40 pounds a year simply to enter the addresses of its outgoing letters in a book, and post them when he had completed this ceremony. After a spell of this he might hope to be transferred to another sphere of bank life and thought, and at the end of his first year he might even hope for a rise in his salary of ten pounds, if his conduct was good, and he had not been late on more than twenty mornings in the year. I am aware that in a properly-regulated story of school-life Walton would have gone to the Eckleton races, returned in a state of speechless intoxication, and been summarily expelled; but facts are facts, and must not be tampered with. The ingenious but not industrious Perry had been superannuated. For three years he had been in the Lower Fourth. Probably the master of that form went to the Head, and said that his constitution would not stand another year of him, and that either he or Perry must go. So Perry had departed. Like a poor play, he had "failed to attract," and was withdrawn. There was also another departure of an even more momentous nature.

Mr Kay had left Eckleton.

Kennedy was no longer head of Kay's. He was now head of Dencroft's.

Mr Dencroft was one of the most popular masters in the school. He was a keen athlete and a tactful master. Fenn and Kennedy knew him well, through having played at the nets and in scratch games with him. They both liked him. If Kennedy had had to select a house-master, he would have chosen Mr Blackburn first. But Mr Dencroft would have been easily second.

Fenn learned the facts from the matron, and detailed them to Kennedy.

"Kay got the offer of a headmastership at a small school in the north, and jumped at it. I pity the fellows there. They are going to have a lively time."

"I'm jolly glad Dencroft has got the house," said Kennedy. "We might have had some awful rotter put in. Dencroft will help us buck up the house games."

The new house-master sent for Kennedy on the first evening of term. He wished to find out how the Head of the house and the ex-Head stood with regard to one another. He knew the circumstances, and comprehended vaguely that there had been trouble.

"I hope we shall have a good term," he said.

"I hope so, sir," said Kennedy.

"You—er—you think the house is keener, Kennedy, than when you first came in?"

"Yes, sir. They are getting quite keen now. We might win the sports."

"I hope we shall. I wish we could win the football cup, too, but I am afraid Mr Blackburn's are very heavy metal."

"It's hardly likely we shall have very much chance with them; but we might get into the final!"

"It would be an excellent thing for the house if we could. I hope Fenn is helping you get the team into shape?" he added.

"Oh, yes, sir," said Kennedy. "We share the captaincy. We both sign the lists."

"A very good idea," said Mr Dencroft, relieved. "Good night, Kennedy."

"Good night, sir," said Kennedy.

122

XXIII

THE HOUSE-MATCHES

The chances of Kay's in the inter-house Football Competition were not thought very much of by their rivals. Of late years each of the other houses had prayed to draw Kay's for the first round, it being a certainty that this would mean that they got at least into the second round, and so a step nearer the cup. Nobody, however weak compared to Blackburn's, which was at the moment the crack football house, ever doubted the result of a match with Kay's. It was looked on as a sort of gentle trial trip.

But the efforts of the two captains during the last weeks of the winter term had put a different complexion on matters. Football is not like cricket. It is a game at which anybody of average size and a certain amount of pluck can make himself at least moderately proficient. Kennedy, after consultations with Fenn, had picked out what he considered the best fifteen, and the two set themselves to knock it into shape. In weight there was not much to grumble at. There were several heavy men in the scrum. If only these could be brought to use their weight to the last ounce when shoving, all would be well as far as the forwards were concerned. The outsides were not so satisfactory. With the exception, of course, of Fenn, they lacked speed. They were well-meaning, but they could not run any faster by virtue of that. Kay's would have to trust to its scrum to pull it through. Peel, the sprinter whom Kennedy had discovered in his search for athletes, had to be put in the pack on account of his weight, which deprived the three-quarter line of what would have been a good man in that position. It was a drawback, too, that Fenn was accustomed to play on the wing. To be of real service, a wing three-quarter must be fed by his centres, and, unfortunately, there was no centre in Kay's—or Dencroft's, as it should now be called— who was capable of making openings enough to give Fenn a chance. So he had to play in the centre, where he did not know the game so well.

Kennedy realised at an early date that the one chance of the house was to get together before the house-matches and play as a coherent

123

team, not as a collection of units. Combination will often make up for lack of speed in a three-quarter line. So twice a week Dencroft's turned out against scratch teams of varying strength.

It delighted Kennedy to watch their improvement. The first side they played ran through them to the tune of three goals and four tries to a try, and it took all the efforts of the Head of the house to keep a spirit of pessimism from spreading in the ranks. Another frost of this sort, and the sprouting keenness of the house would be nipped in the bud. He conducted himself with much tact. Another captain might have made the fatal error of trying to stir his team up with pungent abuse. He realised what a mistake this would be. It did not need a great deal of discouragement to send the house back to its old slack ways. Another such defeat, following immediately in the footsteps of the first, and they would begin to ask themselves what was the good of mortifying the flesh simply to get a licking from a scratch team by twenty-four points. Kay's, they would feel, always had got beaten, and they always would, to the end of time. A house that has once got thoroughly slack does not change its views of life in a moment.

Kennedy acted craftily.

"You played jolly well," he told his despondent team, as they trooped off the field. "We haven't got together yet, that's all. And it was a hot side we were playing today. They would have licked Blackburn's."

A good deal more in the same strain gave the house team the comfortable feeling that they had done uncommonly well to get beaten by only twenty-four points. Kennedy fostered the delusion, and in the meantime arranged with Mr Dencroft to collect fifteen innocents and lead them forth to be slaughtered by the house on the following Friday. Mr Dencroft entered into the thing with a relish. When he showed Kennedy the list of his team on the Friday morning, that diplomatist chuckled. He foresaw a good time in the near future. "You must play up like the dickens," he told the house during the dinner-hour. "Dencroft is bringing a hot lot this afternoon. But I think we shall lick them."

They did. When the whistle blew for No-side, the house had just finished scoring its fourteenth try. Six goals and eight tries to nil was the exact total. Dencroft's returned to headquarters, asking itself in a dazed way if these things could be. They saw that cup on their mantelpiece already. Keenness redoubled. Football became the fashion in Dencroft's. The play of the team improved weekly. And its spirit improved too. The next scratch team they played beat them by a goal and a try to a goal. Dencroft's was not depressed. It put the result down to a fluke. Then they beat another side by a try to nothing; and by that time they had got going as an organised team, and their heart was in the thing.

They had improved out of all knowledge when the house-matches began. Blair's was the lucky house that drew against them in the first round.

"Good business," said the men of Blair. "Wonder who we'll play in the second round."

They left the field marvelling. For some unaccountable reason, Dencroft's had flatly refused to act in the good old way as a doormat for their opponents. Instead, they had played with a dash and knowledge of the game which for the first quarter of an hour quite unnerved Blair's. In that quarter of an hour they scored three times, and finished the game with two goals and three tries to their name.

The School looked on it as a huge joke. "Heard the latest?" friends would say on meeting one another the day after the game. "Kay's—I mean Dencroft's—have won a match. They simply sat on Blair's. First time they've ever won a house-match, I should think. Blair's are awfully sick. We shall have to be looking out."

Whereat the friend would grin broadly. The idea of Dencroft's making a game of it with his house tickled him.

When Dencroft's took fifteen points off Mulholland's, the joke began to lose its humour.

"Why, they must be some good," said the public, startled at the novelty of the idea. "If they win another match, they'll be in the final!"

Kay's in the final! Cricket? Oh, yes, they had got into the final at cricket, of course. But that wasn't the house. It was Fenn. Footer was different. One man couldn't do everything there. The only possible explanation was that they had improved to an enormous extent.

Then people began to remember that they had played in scratch

125

games against the house. There seemed to be a tremendous number of fellows who had done this. At one time or another, it seemed, half the School had opposed Dencroft's in the ranks of a scratch side. It began to dawn on Eckleton that in an unostentatious way Dencroft's had been putting in about seven times as much practice as any other three houses rolled together. No wonder they combined so well.

When the School House, with three first fifteen men in its team, fell before them, the reputation of Dencroft's was established. It had reached the final, and only Blackburn's stood now between it and the cup.

All this while Blackburn's had been doing what was expected of them by beating each of their opponents with great ease. There was nothing sensational about this as there was in the case of Dencroft's. The latter were, therefore, favourites when the two teams lined up against one another in the final. The School felt that a house that had had such a meteoric flight as Dencroft's must—by all that was dramatic—carry the thing through to its obvious conclusion, and pull off the final.

But Fenn and Kennedy were not so hopeful. A certain amount of science, a great deal of keenness, and excellent condition, had carried them through the other rounds in rare style, but, though they would probably give a good account of themselves, nobody who considered the two teams impartially could help seeing that Dencroft's was a weaker side than Blackburn's. Nothing but great good luck could bring them out victorious today.

And so it proved. Dencroft's played up for all they were worth from the kick-off to the final solo on the whistle, but they were over-matched. Blackburn's scrum was too heavy for them, with its three first fifteen men and two seconds. Dencroft's pack were shoved off the ball time after time, and it was only keen tackling that kept the score down. By half-time Blackburn's were a couple of tries ahead. Fenn scored soon after the interval with a great run from his own twenty-five, and for a quarter of an hour it looked as if it might be anybody's game. Kennedy converted the try, so that Blackburn's only led by a single point. A fluky kick or a mistake on the part of a Blackburnite outside might give Dencroft's the cup.

But the Blackburn outsides did not make mistakes. They played a strong, sure game, and the forwards fed them well. Ten minutes before No-side, Jimmy Silver ran in, increasing the lead to six points. And though Dencroft's never went to pieces, and continued to show fight to the very end, Blackburn's were not to be denied, and Challis scored a final try in the corner. Blackburn's won the cup by the comfortable, but not excessive, margin of a goal and three tries to a goal.

Dencroft's had lost the cup; but they had lost it well. Their credit had increased in spite of the defeat.

"I thought we shouldn't be able to manage Blackburn's," said Kennedy, "What we must do now is win that sports' cup."

XXIV

THE SPORTS

There were certain houses at Eckleton which had, as it were, specialised in certain competitions. Thus, Gay's, who never by any chance survived the first two rounds of the cricket and football housers, invariably won the shooting shield. All the other houses sent their brace of men to the range to see what they could do, but every year it was the same. A pair of weedy obscurities from Gay's would take the shield by a comfortable margin. In the same way Mulholland's had only won the cricket cup once since they had become a house, but they had carried off the swimming cup three years in succession, and six years in all out of the last eight. The sports had always been looked on as the perquisite of the School House; and this year, with Milligan to win the long distances, and Maybury the high jump and the weight, there did not seem much doubt at their success. These two alone would pile up fifteen points. Three points were given for a win, two for second place, and one for third. It was this that encouraged Kennedy in the hope that Dencroft's might have a chance. Nobody in the house could beat Milligan or Maybury, but the School House second and third strings were not so invincible. If Dencroft's, by means of second and third places in the long races and the other events which were certainties for their opponents, could hold the School House, Fenn's sprinting might just give them the cup. In the meantime they trained hard, but in an unobtrusive fashion which aroused no fear in School House circles.

The sports were fixed for the last Saturday of term, but not all the races were run on that day. The half-mile came off on the previous Thursday, and the long steeplechase on the Monday after.

The School House won the half-mile, as they were expected to do. Milligan led from the start, increased his lead at the end of the first lap, doubled it half-way through the second, and finally, with a dazzling sprint in the last seventy yards, lowered the Eckleton record by a second and three-fifths, and gave his house three points. Kennedy, who stuck gamely to his man for half the first lap, was beaten on the tape by Crake, of Mulholland's. When sports' day came, therefore, the score was School House three points, Mulholland's two, Dencroft's one. The success of Mulholland's in the half was to the advantage of Dencroft's. Mulholland's was not likely to score many more points, and a place to them meant one or two points less to the School House.

The sports opened all in favour of Dencroft's, but those who knew drew no great consolation from this. School sports always begin with the sprints, and these were Dencroft's certainties. Fenn won the hundred yards as easily as Milligan had won the half. Peel was second, and a Beddell's man got third place. So that Dencroft's had now six points to their rival's three. Ten minutes later they had increased their lead by winning the first two places at throwing the cricket ball, Fenn's throw beating Kennedy's by ten yards, and Kennedy's being a few feet in front of Jimmy Silver's, which, by gaining third place, represented the only point Blackburn's managed to amass during the afternoon.

It now began to dawn upon the School House that their supremacy was seriously threatened. Dencroft's, by its success in the football competition, had to a great extent lived down the reputation the house had acquired when it had been Kay's, but even now the notion of its winning a cup seemed somehow vaguely improper. But the fact had to be faced that it now led by eleven points to the School House's three.

"It's all right," said the School House, "our spot events haven't come off yet. Dencroft's can't get much more now."

And, to prove that they were right, the gap between the two scores began gradually to be filled up. Dencroft's struggled hard, but the School House total crept up and up. Maybury brought it to six by winning the high jump. This was only what had been expected of him. The discomforting part of the business was that the other two places were filled by Morrell, of Mulholland's, and Smith, of Daly's. And when, immediately afterwards, Maybury won the weight, with another School House man second, leaving Dencroft's with third place only, things began to look black for the latter. They were now only one point ahead, and there was the mile to come: and Milligan could give any Dencroftian a hundred yards at that distance.

But to balance the mile there was the quarter, and in the mile Kennedy contrived to beat Crake by much the same number of feet

129

as Crake had beaten him by in the half. The scores of the two houses were now level, and a goodly number of the School House certainties were past.

Dencroft's forged ahead again by virtue of the quarter-mile. Fenn won it; Peel was second; and a dark horse from Denny's got in third. With the greater part of the sports over, and a lead of five points to their name, Dencroft's could feel more comfortable. The hurdle-race was productive of some discomfort. Fenn should have won it, as being blessed with twice the pace of any of his opponents. But Maybury, the jumper, made up for lack of pace by the scientific way in which he took his hurdles, and won off him by a couple of feet. Smith, Dencroft's second string, finished third, thus leaving the totals unaltered by the race.

By this time the public had become alive to the fact that Dencroft's were making a great fight for the cup. They had noticed that Dencroft's colours always seemed to be coming in near the head of the procession, but the School House had made the cup so much their own, that it took some time for the school to realise that another house—especially the late Kay's—was running them hard for first place. Then, just before the hurdle-race, fellows with "correct cards" hastily totted up the points each house had won up-to-date. To the general amazement it was found that, while the School House had fourteen, Dencroft's had reached nineteen, and, barring the long run to be decided on the Monday, there was nothing now that the School House must win without dispute.

A house that will persist in winning a cup year after year has to pay for it when challenged by a rival. Dencroft's instantly became warm favourites. Whenever Dencroft's brown and gold appeared at the scratch, the school shouted for it wildly till the event was over. By the end of the day the totals were more nearly even, but Dencroft's were still ahead. They had lost on the long jump, but not unexpectedly. The totals at the finish were, School House twenty-three, Dencroft's twenty-five. Everything now depended on the long run.

"We might do it," said Kennedy to Fenn, as they changed. "Milligan's a cert for three points, of course, but if we can only get two we win the cup."

"There's one thing about the long run," said Fenn; "you never quite know what's going to happen. Milligan might break down over one of the hedges or the brook. There's no telling."

Kennedy felt that such a remote possibility was something of a broken reed to lean on. He had no expectation of beating the School House long distance runner, but he hoped for second place; and second place would mean the cup, for there was nobody to beat either himself or Crake.

The distance of the long run was as nearly as possible five miles. The course was across country to the village of Ledby in a sort of semicircle of three and a half miles, and then back to the school gates by road. Every Eckletonian who ran at all knew the route by heart. It was the recognised training run if you wanted to train particularly hard. If you did not, you took a shorter spin. At the milestone nearest the school—it was about half a mile from the gates—a good number of fellows used to wait to see the first of the runners and pace their men home. But, as a rule, there were few really hot finishes in the long run. The man who got to Ledby first generally kept the advantage, and came in a long way ahead of the field.

On this occasion the close fight Kennedy and Crake had had in the mile and the half, added to the fact that Kennedy had only to get second place to give Dencroft's the cup, lent a greater interest to the race than usual. The crowd at the milestone was double the size of the one in the previous year, when Milligan had won for the first time. And when, amidst howls of delight from the School House, the same runner ran past the stone with his long, effortless stride, before any of the others were in sight, the crowd settled down breathlessly to watch for the second man.

Then a yell, to which the other had been nothing, burst from the School House as a white figure turned the corner. It was Crake. Waddling rather than running, and breathing in gasps; but still Crake. He toiled past the crowd at the milestone.

"By Jove, he looks bad," said someone.

And, indeed, he looked very bad. But he was ahead of Kennedy. That was the great thing.

He had passed the stone by thirty yards, when the cheering broke out again. Kennedy this time, in great straits, but in better shape than Crake. Dencroft's in a body trotted along at the side of the road, shouting as they went. Crake, hearing the shouts, looked round, almost fell, and then pulled himself together and staggered on again. There were only a hundred yards to go now, and the school gates were in sight at the end of a long lane of spectators. They looked to Kennedy like two thick, black hedges. He could not sprint, though a hundred voices were shouting to him to do so. It was as much as he could do to keep moving. Only his will enabled him to run now. He meant to get to the gates, if he had to crawl.

The hundred yards dwindled to fifty, and he had diminished Crake's lead by a third. Twenty yards from the gates, and he was only half-a-dozen yards behind.

Crake looked round again, and this time did what he had nearly done before. His legs gave way; he rolled over; and there he remained, with the School House watching him in silent dismay, while Kennedy went on and pitched in a heap on the other side of the gates.

"Feeling bad?" said Jimmy Silver, looking in that evening to make inquiries.

"I'm feeling good," said Kennedy.

"That the cup?" asked Jimmy.

Kennedy took the huge cup from the table.

"That's it. Milligan has just brought it round. Well, they can't say they haven't had their fair share of it. Look here. School House. School House. School House. School House. Daly's. School House. Denny's. School House. School House. Ad infinitum."

They regarded the trophy in silence.

"First pot the house has won," said Kennedy at length. "The very first."

"It won't be the last," returned Jimmy Silver, with decision.